W9-BPP-278

WANTED

**Center Point
Large Print**

**This Large Print Book carries the
Seal of Approval of N.A.V.H.**

WANTED

Sisters *of the* Heart

BOOK TWO

SHELLEY SHEPARD GRAY

CENTER POINT PUBLISHING
THORNDIKE, MAINE

This Center Point Large Print edition
is published in the year 2009 by arrangement with
Avon Inspire, an imprint of HarperCollins Publishers.

The text of this Large Print edition is unabridged.
In other aspects, this book may vary
from the original edition.
Printed in the United States of America.
Set in 16-point Times New Roman type.

ISBN: 978-1-60285-464-2

Library of Congress Cataloging-in-Publication Data

Gray, Shelley Shepard.
    Wanted : sisters of the heart / Shelley Shepard Gray.
        p. cm.
    ISBN 978-1-60285-464-2 (library binding : alk. paper)
    1. Amish--Fiction. 2. Bed and breakfast accommodations--Fiction. 3. Widowers--
Fiction. 4. Single fathers--Fiction. 5. Large type books. I. Title.

PS3607.R3966W36 2009b
813'.6--dc22

2009000444

This is the day which the Lord has made.
Let us rejoice and be glad in it.

Psalm 118:24

We did not inherit this land from our fathers.
We are borrowing it from our children.

Amish Proverb

Chapter 1

Katie Brenneman noticed that Jonathan Lundy was crushing the brim of his hat. Round and round he turned it, fingering the black felt as he spoke. Every few moments, without warning, his fingers would clench and the rim would succumb to his grip.

If he continued the process much longer, Jonathan was going to be in dire need of a new hat.

"Katie, are you listening, Daughter?"

She started, daring to glance at her mother, who was sitting across from her on the love seat, her current sewing project forgotten in the basket next to her. "Yes, *Mamm*. I'm listening."

"You have hardly looked at our guest once since he's arrived. You haven't spoken more than a few words." Her mother treated Katie to a look she knew well. It said she had better shape up and soon. "Is everything all right?"

Irene Brenneman was a lot of things, but a fool certainly wasn't one of them. Katie swallowed. "Of course."

"Then you are interested in what Jonathan has to say?"

Katie had been fond of Jonathan Lundy for years. She'd always been mighty interested in what he had to say. Not that he seemed to notice. "Yes."

The hat took another beating as Jonathan spoke. "I have something to ask of Katie. Something that I am hoping she would think was a mighty *gut* idea."

Now Katie was all ears. Had Jonathan finally seen her as she wished? As a woman available for courting? Stilling herself, she inhaled.

Her mother's cheeks pinkened. "What was your idea, Jonathan?"

He swallowed uncomfortably. "I'm . . . I'm hopin' Katie—that Katie . . ."

Her mother leaned forward. "Yes?"

"Well, I'm in need of Katie here to help with my daughters."

Her *daed* coughed. "With your daughters?"

Crunch! went the brim again. "*Jah*. Just while my sister Winnie goes to Indiana for a bit."

Katie exhaled swiftly. Well, she'd certainly been mistaken! Jonathan had been thinking of her, but not as a future bride. Oh no. As a nursemaid for his five- and seven-year-old daughters.

"For how long?" her father asked. Usually, he joked around, or whittled on one of the many canes he was famous for creating. Now, though, he only sat solemnly, his expression grave.

"Two months."

Two months of living at Jonathan Lundy's home? Of caring for his daughters like their mother. Of seeing to his household, making his meals, cleaning his home. As a wife would do.

After a long moment of thoughtful silence, her

father said, "Two months is a long time, I'm thinkin'."

"I know it."

Oh! Jonathan Lundy still hadn't looked her way! Katie bristled. She hated being talked over like she had nothing to say for herself.

Though she surely didn't like the sound of this conversation, either. She was about to speak her mind when her mother spoke.

"Mary and Hannah are nice girls, to be sure. And they are a pleasure to be around."

Jonathan nodded. His expression relaxed. For the first time since he'd arrived, the hat hung limply in his hand. "Thank you. Ever since my Sarah died, I've had a time of it."

My Sarah. Those words told Katie everything she needed to know. Jonathan might never think of anyone other than Sarah. Ever.

Her mother winced. "Sarah's accident was a tragedy, we all know that. But you and your sister, Winnie, are raisin' the girls just fine. I know Mary has missed her mother something awful, and it wasn't easy when young Hannah was still little more than a babe."

Jonathan's face became expressionless. "Neither Mary nor Hannah understood death at first. Hannah woke up crying for her mother more often than not, and Mary . . ." His voice lowered. "Well, Mary refused to ride in a buggy for months after the accident. But they're better now."

"Yes, indeed. I know they are better." Her mother paused, as if measuring her words. "But, you see, I don't think it would be right for our Katie to take on such a job."

Her father slapped his hands on his thighs. "Not at all. This job you speak of is not the one for Katie."

"If you're worried I would take advantage of her, I promise I will do no such thing. I'll move to the *daadi haus* and be always respectful."

"We are sure you will."

"And I will pay her, too. Please don't think I wanted Katie to work for nothing."

This conversation was getting worse and worse. It was so uncomfortable that Katie no longer minded that they were speaking about her as if she wasn't there. She didn't want to be there.

"Money is not the problem, Jonathan," her mother said sternly.

The decision had clearly been made. Katie didn't know whether to be thankful or disappointed. Here was her opportunity to show Jonathan just what kind of mother and wife she could be. Here was her chance! But it was also a risk that Jonathan would only see her as a caregiver for his girls.

And though she'd always wanted to be a wonderful *gut* mother and housewife, she wanted to be valued as *Katie*. As someone special. Perhaps that would never happen in Jonathan's home.

Jonathan looked surprised. "Oh. I see. I was just

thinking that you might have an extra hand, now that Anna Metzger is living here."

Katie smiled at the mention of her best friend's name. Anna had been living at their inn for seven months now, and quite an adjustment it had been! Her dear friend was determined to learn the ways of the Amish, join the church, and eventually exchange vows with Henry, Katie's brother.

Katie's father spoke. "Anna is a great help, to be sure. But that isn't the problem."

"What is?"

With a tender look her way, her mother spoke. "It would be improper for Katie to live with you, that way."

"In what way? She'd only be caring for the girls."

With a hint of censure in her tone, her mother said, "She is a young woman of marriageable age, Jonathan. Certainly you agree?"

For the first time since he'd arrived, Jonathan looked at her hard. From top to bottom. Katie did her best to sit still, chin up, as if she didn't mind being stared at like a horse at market.

Jonathan's hat fell, whether the brim gave out or he was startled, Katie didn't know. But, he did look mighty flustered. His brow was damp as he reached down to pick the hat up.

The tension in the room increased. Helplessly, Katie turned to her mother. *Say something!* she ordered silently. *Say something to make things better!*

But her mother remained silent. Her father shot her a troubled glance but merely waited for Jonathan to respond.

He finally did . . . very slowly. "Th- . . . though Katie seems . . . Is. Mighty nice . . ." He shifted. Pulled at his shirt. "I'm not in the market for a new wife, you see."

Her *mamm* raised a brow. "Ever? All girls need a mother." Gently, she added, "Perhaps one day you might even find yourself eager for a wife."

Jonathan looked awkwardly at the floor.

Katie felt stung. Had Jonathan become so terribly entrenched in his world of loneliness that he didn't even see that chance of future happiness?

"I've heard enough. I'm sorry, but we canna allow Katie to live there, with you." Her father stood up with a groan. "Now, I best get to work, there's a lot of things that need doing."

"I wish you would reconsider," Jonathan interrupted quickly. "There's really no one else to turn to."

"That may be the case, but honestly, Jonathan, we have Katie to look after. Don'tcha see?"

Jonathan stood up, his expression grim. "I see. I see that I shouldn't have asked for so much."

To Katie's surprise, neither parent refuted Jonathan's words. Instead, her father merely walked him to the door, then followed him outside.

A feeling of loss flowed through her. Well, there was her chance, and it had come and gone in mere minutes. As they heard Jonathan's buggy roll down their gravel drive, Katie turned to her mother. "I feel sorry for him. Jonathan is a proud man. It had to be difficult to ask for help."

Her mother picked up her sewing again. "We both know pride is a sin, Katie. He will be fine. It is far better if you stay here at home. Where we can keep a close eye on you."

Katie felt her insides come apart. All at once, the true reason for her parents' reluctance for her to be at the Lundys' began to dawn on her. Her parents were not concerned with Jonathan's behavior.

They were far more worried about her own. Perhaps her past mistakes were not as swept aside as she'd thought. "I'm twenty years old, you know."

"Just twenty. Your birthday was only two weeks ago."

"I'm just sayin' that twenty is much older than sixteen."

Her mother jabbed her needle through the fabric. "That is true."

"What do you think Jonathan will do now?"

"It is not our concern."

"But Winnie really wants to go to Indiana. She told me she can't wait to go. And, well, she doesn't get to take time for herself very often. The only instance I recall her asking for a break was last spring, when Anna had first come to live with us."

"Winnie's caring for her brother's children. She

shouldn't need breaks from that. It's best that she concentrate on her duties, Katie. We both know what can happen when duty is forgotten."

Katie glanced at her mother again. Her mother's shoulders were stiff, her posture rigid. With great effort, Katie tried to stop her hands from shaking. What could her mother know?

"I'm going to go check on Anna," she said, abruptly scurrying from the room.

Miraculously, her mother let her go without a word.

But as Katie rounded the corner and faced the beautiful front staircase, she knew she couldn't visit her best friend just then. She didn't want to burden Anna with her troubles, or be surrounded by her joyful nature. Yes, lately, Anna had been very joyful.

She'd had every reason to be. Anna was unofficially courting Katie's brother, Henry. She was also in the process of learning everything she could about the Amish and practicing her Pennsylvania Dutch, all in preparation to join the church.

Bypassing the stairs, Katie threw open the door and strode outside, just as quickly as her feet could take her.

The mid-October sunshine brought welcome rays of warmth to the blustery air. As the multitude of crisp yellow, orange, and red leaves crunched underfoot, Katie took a moment to quiet down. To remind herself that she was safe.

Just as she closed her eyes to pray for guidance, a fierce yip of a small black-and-white pup caught her attention.

There, at front of the whitewashed two-story barn sat her brother, a wiggly puppy in his arms.

Katie hurried closer. "Henry, whatever are you doing with that dog?"

His smile was broad and transformed his usual solemn expression. "Caleb Miller's Daisy had a litter. He gave me a pup in exchange for the work I did in his shop last Friday and Saturday."

Unable to help herself, Katie reached out for the pup, then carefully cradled him in her arms. After a bit of squirming, the puppy leaned closer and licked her face. "Oh, he's *wunderbaar schee*— wonderful nice, that's for sure. What are you going to do with him? Is he for Anna?"

"No. She's got enough to do, with the inn and her lessons," he said easily.

Her brother used to take everything seriously and saw little humor in even the silliest of things. His relationship with Anna changed all that. Now the two of them were entering into a bond that went beyond all their cultural differences. Each was becoming a stronger person because of it.

"This puppy is for you."

"Truly? Why?"

Looking suddenly bashful, Henry shrugged. "I don't know. Maybe because you love puppies so?"

She was prevented from replying when the puppy

wriggled some more and yipped out his own reply. "Oh, he's a dear. Look how he has three black paws and one white one." The puppy yipped again and stretched two paws, just like he was showing them off. Katie couldn't keep the smile from her face.

Henry laughed. "I think the two of you will get along just fine."

"Do *Mamm* and *Daed* know?"

"*Jah*, they know." Scratching the pup on its head, he said, "Don't worry so, Katie." Motioning to the open windows of their house, he murmured, "I overheard some of Jonathan's visit."

Katie avoided his eyes. "I don't know what I'm supposed to do with my life."

Henry clicked his tongue. "You will. What's meant to be will happen. It always does."

"I hope so." Even though she knew she'd regret scrubbing the stains out later, Katie sat down on the dusty ground to let the pup scamper. He leaped from her lap, sniffed impatiently around the area, then eagerly ran to her again, his tail wagging like they hadn't seen each other in days.

He'd come back to her. He hadn't chased after Henry. Though she knew it was a silly thing to be happy about, Katie was pleased. Perhaps everything did work out the way it was supposed to. Perhaps everything with Jonathan Lundy would work out one way or another, as well.

Perhaps one day, her past would finally stay in the past.

Finding comfort in prayer, she whispered, "Dear Lord, my gracious God, please help me remember how far I've come from my past. Please help me remember to enjoy the present. And please help me see where my future lies. I do so want to follow your will."

With all her heart, Katie did want to follow where the Lord intended to lead her. She knew she did.

So why was she always wishing and hoping for things that could never be?

"Anna, you must be careful filling the jars," Katie cautioned four days later, as she carefully lifted the jar out of the boiling water then poured exactly one cup of preserves into the glass container. "If you are not careful, you're going to fill them too much and then they won't seal properly."

Anna pursed her lips. "I thought this was supposed to be an easy job."

"It is." Katie had been helping can since she was old enough to scrub vegetables. She found it awfully strange that Anna had reached adulthood hardly knowing how to take care of a house and home. "Canning is a most agreeable chore, to be sure."

Anna held up a finger. "Not for me. Look at my fingers." She held a finger up for inspection while blowing on it so hard the paper behind her fluttered on the counter. "Do you see the blisters? They really hurt. I got burned when the boiling jam got the best of me."

Katie had nothing to say to that. The blisters would teach her to be more careful in the future. But she didn't have to say a single word because Henry entered the roomy kitchen and made a beeline for Anna.

He frowned as soon as he noticed her pained expression. "Anna, you hurt yourself?"

Just like a child, she held up a finger. "It's nothing. Merely a blister."

"It looks terribly painful, though."

Anna nodded. "It is."

To Katie's chagrin, her older brother carefully pressed Anna's fingers to his lips before leading her to the sink. And Anna, why she was letting him lead her around! As Katie watched her brother coddle her best friend, she could barely hold her patience. Anna had suffered a tiny burn, not a disastrous accident! Oh, she had much to learn. No self-respecting Amish woman would fuss over a burn so much.

She was just about to mention that when she realized neither Henry nor Anna would notice if she spoke at all. They were standing in front of the sink, cool water running, lost in each other's eyes.

Suddenly, it was too warm to be there with them. Too confining. Too much.

"I'm going to check on Roman," she said, anxious to see the new puppy.

Neither looked her way.

Frustrated, Katie ran out to the pen that Henry had made for the puppy. He wiggled with delight when he saw her and yipped. She opened the gate, freed him, then sat on the ground as he jumped and played all around her. But to her surprise, even the bundle of black-and-white fur didn't lift her spirits.

No, he only reminded her that she had no special person of her own. And, unfortunately, that she had once had someone who had cared for her very much. He'd cared for her and she'd pushed him away.

Her mother, who'd been out feeding the goats, slowly approached. "I do believe this is the first time I've not seen you laugh and giggle at this puppy's antics."

Her mother made her sound awfully young. "I need more than just puppies, *Mamm*. I am older now, remember?"

"*Ach*, Katie, you are surely havin' a time of it, aren't you now?"

Katie scrambled to her feet and followed her mother back to the goats' pen. "I'm all right."

"Come now, I saw you running out here. What is wrong?"

"I don't know." How could she ever put into words everything she was thinking? She could never admit to her mother all the selfish and confusing thoughts that were brewing inside of her.

Her mother nodded to Katie's hand. "Come now, something's wrong. Look what you are doing! We both know you would never pet Gertie without a reason."

That was unfortunately true. Oh, how she'd always hated those ornery goats. She had ever since they'd gotten loose one fine spring day and found her first Log Cabin quilt on the line. In a matter of minutes, Billie and Gertie had chewed on that quilt, making a mess of years of careful hard work.

Because her mother was patiently waiting for an answer, Katie gave her one. "It's nothing. Anna and Henry looked like they needed a moment or two of privacy."

"I suppose a courting couple needs a moment or two from time to time." Looking toward the house, she wrinkled her brow. "I thought you were working on jam this morning. Did you already fill the jars?"

"No. We had to take a break when Anna burned her fingers." Unable to stop the flow of words any longer, Katie blurted, "The way she carried on, you would think her finger was on fire. And of course, it happened just when Henry was coming in for some lemonade. The moment he saw her he rushed over and put her fingers under the water." Katie didn't even feel like mentioning how Henry had kissed Anna's fingers, too.

"That was good thinkin'."

"But that isn't the point! Anna could've tended to a blister by herself. She didn't need to act so helpless around my brother."

"*Ah.*"

Katie ignored her mother's smile and continued. "As a matter of fact, she wouldn't even have been burned if she would have listened to me and been more careful." Thinking again to how long it was taking to can preserves, Katie felt her temper explode. "Anna doesn't listen, *Mamm*! I've told her time and again to only fill the jars two-thirds of the way full, but she always ignores my suggestions."

"I doubt she ignores you on purpose. This is all new for her."

"Everything is new, even after being here seven months. She is helpless."

"She's accomplished in other ways."

"But that hardly matters now. Amish women need to know how to can."

"And she will learn," her mother soothed. "We all learn what we need to learn in our own time, don'tcha think?"

Now that her temper had calmed, Katie felt embarrassed for her behavior and cross words. Her mother was exactly right. Anna was doing the best that she could. "I'm sorry."

"I'm not sorry that you're sharing your thoughts with me. Come now, what is really bothering you?"

Katie knew she couldn't keep all her mixed up feelings inside any longer. And, because she trusted her mother's advice more than anyone else's, she whispered, "Anna is getting everything I've wanted."

Her mother's lips twitched. "You've wanted to burn yourself canning?"

"No, of course not." Reluctantly, she mumbled, "Soon Anna will have a husband."

"*Ah.* You are still thinking of Jonathan Lundy and his offer."

She couldn't help herself. For the last few days, it was all she ever thought about. "I want to go to Jonathan's house, *Mamm.*"

"Staying in his home and watching over his girls does not seem like a terribly wise decision, especially if you have a fondness for Jonathan."

"You knew I cared for him?"

"I would have had to be blind and dumb not to know that, Katie." Leading the way out of the goats' pen, she turned to her. "I'm sorry to say this, but the fact is that he does not feel the same way. He might never feel that way. Everyone knows he misses Sarah. You'll be setting yourself up for heartache."

"Then let me have heartache while I'm at least trying. My heart already hurts now and I've done nothing." All she'd been doing for months was helping her friend learn the Amish ways.

"I see." After looking at Katie once again, her

mother picked up her skirts and shook them. "I'll do some more thinking about this. In the meantime, go see to Anna." With a bit of a smile she said, "I do believe Henry left her, so she's all alone in the kitchen once again."

Katie could only imagine what Anna was doing if she still wasn't nursing a hurt finger. "No telling what mess she's made now."

"Thank goodness she has you to show her the best way to clean things up, yes?"

Katie couldn't think of a suitable reply.

Chapter 2

Some days, Jonathan missed Sarah so much he thought his insides would break. Sometimes, he longed for his wife so much, he'd be willing to do just about anything to see her again.

It was one of those days.

Outside the kitchen, the air was crisp and the sky a beautiful robin's-egg blue. The maple near the house was intent to fill the area with its glory . . . the leaves seemed to change to burnt red right before his eyes. Yes, the Lord had blessed them with a perfect late fall day. Within days, the air would become colder and the fields would be covered with a pristine white blanket of snow.

But not quite yet.

When Sarah was alive, she would have been singing a happy tune and would have had every window in their house open to greet the day, regardless of how sharp the wind was. Now he only opened one.

Oh, how he used to grumble about the frostiness of the kitchen. Now, a far different chill permeated the room. One of silence and emptiness. No matter how many people might take up the space, things weren't changing. His wife was gone and in her place was a giant gap of a hole that couldn't seem to be filled.

And he'd tried.

But it was no use. Like a doughnut, there was no center to their lives. The imagery almost made him smile. When Sarah had been alive, he'd taken it for granted that he was the center of the family.

He'd been much mistaken.

Winnie's presence was helping, though lately he'd seen a shadow in her expression. Jonathan knew what the shadow was for. At twenty-two, his sister was yearning for a future of her own. A family and home of her own.

Being his lifeline wasn't giving her the satisfaction he'd hoped it would. If he were honest with himself, he knew he should be happy for his sister. The Lord asked everyone to find a life partner and raise a family. It would be a terrible shame if Winnie did not yearn for those things, too. But oh, he wished she would have chosen to wait a bit longer for his sake.

Outside the window, a pair of cardinals flew by,

the male so proud and bright, his mate's colors far more subdued. Yet together they made a mighty fine pair. Could he fault his sister for wanting what all creatures had?

He could not. But what still remained was his needs. He needed someone to watch his girls while Winnie went to meet her beau.

"I still canna believe that the Brennemans refused you," Winnie stated over her half-drunk tea. "Your idea was most reasonable."

He'd thought so, too. Carefully, he flipped the eggs in the pan, grimacing as yet again one of the yolks broke and ran across the griddle's surface, hardening in seconds. "Not everyone wants to care for another person's children, I suppose."

"No, that's not it." She drummed her fingers on the oak table he'd inherited from their parents. "What did they say again?"

Even though they'd discussed the conversation over and over during the past week, Jonathan dutifully recounted the encounter again. "John and Irene said they did not want their daughter living with me. Alone."

"But you would be with the girls, and in the *daadi haus*, too." Winnie frowned. "And what is with that nonsense, anyway? Don't they realize that your heart has already been taken?"

It had been, indeed. He had loved. Once. And then, to his shame, he'd felt that love fade into something far different. Something that only in the privacy of his thoughts could he admit was disappointment.

Now he only felt guilt for how Sarah died. That guilt weighed heavy on him. Now that it was almost two years since the accident, Jonathan figured he'd be carrying that burden for the rest of his life.

Yes, his heart was locked up somewhere else and wasn't going to escape any time in the near future. Most likely, ever. Katie Brenneman had nothing to be afraid of.

"Between work and the girls I am busy indeed, but I've a feeling that they don't see it that way."

Winnie joined him at the counter. With easy movements, she wiped off the crumbs of her toast as he pulled his own bread from the confines of the oven. "I should go talk to Katie. I'm sure she could talk her parents into changing their decision if she just put her mind to it."

"Winnie, you mustn't. John and Irene have already made their decision." After shaking a healthy amount of pepper on his eggs and placing the toast on top, Jonathan carried his plate to the table. "Maybe, you could put off your trip for a while."

Her hand tightened on the rag. "Don't ask me to do that. I must go to Indiana. I need to go. Malcolm has been so wonderful *gut* in his letters, there might be something between us." More quietly, she added, "I hope there might be."

He said the obvious. "Indiana is far away." And because he wasn't as good a brother as he wished he were, he added quite peevishly, "They may be quite different there, too."

"Like how?"

"I don't know. But different is different."

She shook her head slightly. "Oh, *bruder*. Sometimes different is good. Sometimes change is what the Lord wants."

"Sometimes not."

"Jonathan, once you followed your heart. Now it is time for me to do the same."

He knew she was right. Winnie was a pretty girl, to be sure. Thin as a reed, she used to look somewhat like a beanpole. Now, though, she merely looked slender and feminine. Her light blue eyes emphasized her ivory skin and dark, almost black, hair.

Yes, it was time for Winnie to be thinking of courtship and love. "I hear you."

Looking satisfied that she won, she plopped his hot pan in water. "I'll figure something out for you, I promise. I will not go at the expense of Mary and Hannah. I'd never leave if I didn't feel they were in good hands."

"What are you talking about?" Mary asked, popping her head into the kitchen.

Winnie blushed. "Nothing, child."

"It is something," Mary said in that forthright way of hers. The way that had been Sarah's. Sure, confident. At times too much so. "I heard my name."

"You shouldn't be eavesdropping, Daughter."

Mary crossed her arms over her chest, yet another true imitation of her mother. "I didn't listen on purpose. But I did hear my name."

Slyly, Winnie raised an eyebrow Jonathan's way. Yes, Mary was a handful.

"Your aunt and I were discussing the particulars about Katie coming to live with us," Jonathan finally said.

"Why?"

"Because I am going to go to Indiana for a spell and Katie and I have been friends for a long time." She touched Mary's nose gently. "Since we were your age."

"Why do you want to go away?"

"I'm not going for certain. I just might." Winnie picked up Jonathan's plate and rinsed it off. "Would you like an egg this morning, Mary?"

"No. I just want toast."

"Daughter, you should eat more."

As expected, Mary ignored her father. "Katie hasn't come over lately."

"That's because she's been busy. As have I."

"Well, I don't know her. Not too good."

It didn't escape Jonathan's notice that his daughter wrinkled her nose when she spoke their neighbor's name. "You certainly do too know her."

"Not well. I don't see why we want her here. I don't."

All brusque and business, Winnie shooed Mary

and little Hannah, who'd just appeared, toward the table. "Sit down, now. It is time to eat."

But the ever-curious Hannah stopped in her tracks. "*Who* do we not want here?"

"No one," Winnie said as she shuffled Hannah to the broad oak bench. "I'm making you an egg. Eat some toast while you're waiting."

Obediently, she picked up a piece of toast. But to Jonathan's dismay, Hannah was not to be put off, either. "Who, who, who?"

Just as Jonathan was about to tell the youngest to be quiet, Mary answered. "Katie Brenneman."

Suspiciously quiet, Winnie slipped an egg onto a plate and placed it in front of Hannah.

Hannah looked at them all with wide eyes. "Why don't we want Katie here?"

"I want her here," Winnie said.

"I don't. And you don't either, Hannah," Mary proclaimed.

"Yes, I do. I like Katie." Smiling sweetly, Hannah speared the egg with her fork. "Katie gives me cookies at gatherings. And she always has a friendly smile."

Sounding far older than her years, Mary said, "Cookies do not make for a nice person."

"Why not?"

Jonathan could not take any more. "Katie is indeed a nice person, and that is all we will say about that. It is sinful the way you two are gossiping."

"I'm not gossiping and telling tales," Mary

29

retorted, obviously offended. "I'm only telling you my feelings. Can't I even do that?"

"Of course you can. But you mustn't say those things about Katie."

"Why not? Why must we not have feelings about Katie Brenneman?"

"Daughters, eat your breakfast and get ready for school. We've had enough talk for now, I think."

While Hannah busied herself with butter and jam, Mary narrowed her eyes. "But—"

Winnie turned away from the sink. "Listen to your father, Mary."

As silence filled the room again, Jonathan stood up. "I'm going outside," he murmured as he walked to the hooks by the door. Before any of the girls could ask another question, he slipped on his coat and walked out into the crisp, cool air. Into the type of day that Sarah had always enjoyed.

He'd never told her how much he far preferred the hot, long days of summer.

In fact, he'd never told her much about his tastes and wants. Instead, each had ventured into married life determined to be as busy as possible. Sarah had been terribly independent, always going wherever she needed to go. He'd never thought much about the dangers of her driving the buggy so much.

Maybe if he had, she'd still be with him. Maybe if he'd tried harder to tell her how much he liked her being at home, she'd still be there. But now, of course, it was far too late.

With a sigh, Holly Norris signed the letter with "Your friend, Holly," then slipped the piece of stationery into the envelope and addressed it to the McClusky General Store.

"Well, Brandon, I don't know if Katie will ever see this, but at least I'll know I tried." She looked fondly at her older brother. "Right?"

If Brandon heard, he gave no notice. Today was one of his bad days. Four months ago, he'd been diagnosed with cancer of the liver. Since then, his health had been steadily declining. At first, the doctors had talked about chemotherapy and radiation treatments. But after several scans and exhaustive tests, it was obvious that he was never going to get better. Actually, it was becoming obvious that Holly was about to lose him very soon.

Every time she thought about Brandon dying, Holly choked up. He was the only family she had left. Their mother died of breast cancer four years ago. And their dad—well, neither of them had heard from Graham Norris in almost a decade.

For most of her life, it had only just been she and Brandon.

And lately, it had just been her. She'd never felt so alone.

For a few hours each day, Brandon would regain consciousness. Luckily, she was always there to witness it.

Holly mentally thanked her boss, Dr. Kinter, for allowing her to take a leave of absence from her job as a veterinary assistant. What would she do if Brandon woke up, only to find no one was sitting by his side?

During those moments of consciousness, Holly would try and sound chipper and chatty. For her sake, he would attempt to smile, but they both knew even that effort cost him. Brandon was slipping away. He was losing interest in almost everything in their world, talking more about the past and their mother than Holly could ever remember.

There was only one subject that ever drew a familiar spark into his beautiful hazel eyes—Katie Brenneman.

Almost three years ago, he'd fallen hard for Katie. In return, she'd led him on, then broke his heart. Katie had broken Holly's heart as well. She'd thought they'd been good friends. Best friends.

Then she'd found out that Katie had just been pretending to care about them. She'd never intended to go to trade school with Holly. She'd never intended to one day be roommates like she'd promised. She'd never intended to ever fall in love with Brandon.

No, she was Amish.

To Holly's dismay, Brandon still carried a torch for Katie. And now she was the only person he wanted to see. So Holly was swallowing her pride and doing everything she could to contact Katie.

Even though, really, Holly couldn't care less whether she ever saw Katie again. She didn't appreciate being used.

As the machines clicked and sighed around her brother, Holly nodded to the nurse on duty, then walked to the hospital's front lobby and posted the letter.

The irony of the address didn't escape her. The truth was, even though she'd felt she had become best friends with Katie, the fact remained that really, she hadn't known her very well at all. She didn't know where she lived, only that she shopped at the McClusky General Store.

Oh, and that Katie had lied to them all. About who she was and what her dreams were. About who she loved and what she wanted to be.

As Holly watched the envelope slide down the glass mail slot, she wondered what Katie would do when she saw it. Not wanting to put Brandon's news in the letter, Holly had asked Katie to meet her at the Brown Dog Café. Part of her hoped Katie would ignore the note.

But even though Holly wished that, she hoped and prayed that Katie would rush to Brandon's side. He wanted to see her. He needed to see Katie.

And so, Holly knew she would do whatever it took to give him what he wanted. Even reaching out to the girl she'd hoped to never see again.

Chapter 3

"I know my brother Jonathan's intentions are true. They are without reproach, and without any ulterior motives. Katie's presence is surely needed."

With a sense of alarm, Katie looked at her mother, who was busy frying chicken. Beside her Anna was peeling potatoes. She, herself, was rolling out pie crust. Winnie was pressing some napkins for the evening's meal at the inn.

Though the tasks were mundane and their hands busy and useful, the conversation certainly was not. It seemed to bump along and halt like a wheel stuck in a rut, stopping and starting in rough movements.

Anna looked so ill at ease that she'd most likely peeled more potatoes than they would need over the coming week.

Katie felt her own nerves being pulled as the silence stretched on. "*Mamm*?" she said. "Did you hear?"

"*Ach*. Yes." With a frown, her mother glanced up from the frying pan. "Things are not as simple as you make them seem, Winnie."

"Sometimes they are," Winnie fired back. She placed the hot iron she'd been using back in its holder. Chin up, she looked at them all, her light blue eyes shining, the perfect contrast to her dark-as-night brows and hair. "I think you may be making things too difficult. Jonathan and I need help. That is all. We need another pair of hands."

"You are not asking for only our hands, Winnie. You are asking Katie to live with you."

Katie's cheeks heated. She knew that tone in her mother's voice. It plainly said her patience was wearing thin and to tread lightly.

It was obvious Winnie heard no such warning. Still ignoring her pile of ironing, she crossed her arms over her chest. "I thought your offers of assistance were genuine when Sarah passed on."

Anna groaned and grabbed another potato.

Katie sucked in a breath. Winnie's words were mighty harsh. Of course all of the Brennemans had offered to help back at Sarah's funeral. But helping when they were able and her living with Jonathan were two different things.

"My offer was indeed genuine, Winnie," *Mamm* said quietly. "I have helped your family out time and again over the last year and a half."

Katie kept her head down, concentrating on fluting the pie crust's edges. Oh, her mother was in a fine state. Winnie shouldn't push so.

But still, she did. "It would just be for two months. Let's see, it's the first of November now. In two months, it will be the beginning of January." She pointed to the frosty windowpane, evidence that the weather outside was finally getting colder. "What's two months, after all? The spring crocuses won't even have started to bloom."

"Two months can be a long time if it's the wrong situation."

"I've waited a long time to meet the right man," Winnie said.

Katie's mother clucked. "You will find the right man sooner or later."

Winnie nibbled on a bottom lip. "None of the boys I talked to at singings interested me. No one since, either. Before long, I'm going to be en *altmaedel*."

Katie chuckled in spite of the serious conversation. "You are not an old maid, Winnie. You are hardly more than two years older than me."

"You can't deny it has been a long time since we used to look forward to our Sunday singings. We are not so young anymore."

Katie did remember how much fun she and Winnie used to have together. They'd go to the singings on Sunday evenings, eager to meet other teenagers. Eager to find a special boy.

Unfortunately, neither ever had found anyone special. As the years passed and they attended other friends' weddings, they'd begun to drift apart.

"I feel like an old maid, and that is the truth," Winnie proclaimed. Turning to Katie's mother again, she said, "Are you worried about the girls? Mary can be a handful, but she's a sweet girl at heart."

"It's not the children that concern me, Winnie."

"Then what?" Winnie turned to Anna. "What do you think? This is my time to actually meet

Malcolm. I figured you, if no one else, would understand the obstacles I am facing. It is hard to learn about someone from mere letters."

Anna blushed but said nothing. Only the potato peels flying onto the counter at a frantic pace gave notice to her discomfort.

Words warred inside of Katie. She yearned to push her mother to give in. To let her live with the Lundys. But, she didn't like how Winnie was pressing them, either. Guilt and obligation didn't make a fitting pair.

Once all the chicken was drying on a copy of the *Budget*, her mother sighed. "Tell me about this young man you are writing to."

"He's a Troyer. Malcolm's great-grandmother was Ruth Troyer. Do you know of the family?"

Grudgingly, her mother nodded. "I do. They're good stock."

"I knew it." Winnie's smile, with those perfect dimples, lit up the room. "I could tell from the way he described his family that they were people I would like to know and would get along with."

"Now, I didn't say that, Winnie."

Winnie waved a hand dismissively. "You've said enough. Besides, I know Malcolm quite well now. We've been corresponding for some time."

"Letters don't always tell what matters about a person," Anna interrupted. "It's hard to get a real sense of what a person is like from just a few words, or even a few meetings."

"Malcolm's letters are more than brief messages," Winnie replied. "They're truly thoughtful notes revealing his heart and soul."

Katie bit her lip as she noticed Anna and her mother exchange amused glances.

Seemingly encouraged, Winnie continued. "Our notes to each other are personal and heartfelt. Like there's something between us that's special." She glanced toward Anna, and then finally to Katie. "You both know what that's like, don'tcha?"

"I do," Anna answered as a faint blush stained her cheeks. "Henry and I have written a few notes to each other."

This was news to Katie. "When did my brother write to you?"

"When we were apart." Turning to Winnie, Anna said, "But, Winnie, I must say that nothing takes the place of conversations face-to-face. Whenever Henry is pleased, he gets this crease in between his brows. Now I know when he's tired because he will favor his right leg a bit."

"It never did heal up right after that horse kicked him," Katie's mother commented.

Anna's expression became tender. "Now that Henry and I have gotten to know each other better, I know he and I will make each other happy when we are married. Because we've taken the time to get to know each other better. I . . . I've never felt this way before."

Winnie flicked a snowy white cloth in the air to

snap it open. "See, Mrs. Brenneman? I need to be near Malcolm. I need the time with him, face-to-face."

"I hear what you are saying."

Winnie turned to Katie. "What about you? Have you ever been in love?"

Katie jabbed another pie crust with a fork. "You know I'm not courtin' anyone." Her words exposed everything she'd always wanted to hide deep inside of her. Frustration, wistfulness. Regret.

But Winnie, too intent on her own problems, didn't take notice. "Not even during the singings? Or afterward? I seem to remember you spent quite a bit of time out and about during your *rum*—"

"No," Katie said quickly, cutting Winnie off before she could say a thing about Katie's running-around years. Of her *rumspringa*.

Katie hated to be reminded of that time. Of the things she'd done. Primly, she put a stop to Winnie's sly insinuations. "Everyone experiments a bit during their running-around years. I did nothing out of the ordinary. *Nothing*."

Winnie looked at her in surprise. "I didn't say you did."

"I was baptized and joined the church in June, you know."

"I know." With a half smile, Winnie said, "I was there, remember?"

Just as Katie began to think that perhaps all talk of her past was behind her, Winnie pressed again.

"But what about your time among the English?" she pressed, her voice light and full of mirth. "Tell us the truth. Didn't you ever find an English boy attractive?"

Katie felt all three pairs of eyes turn her way, capturing her with direct stares. Her mother's regard felt hot, like Winnie's forgotten iron, searing the layers of lies she'd cloaked over herself. Anna merely looked curious.

She shifted uncomfortably and stayed focused on the poor pie shell, which had done nothing to deserve her harsh treatment with the fork.

"Do you intend to answer, Katie?" Winnie asked.

"There was no one special."

Winnie raised a brow. "Indeed? I could have sworn I heard you keeping company with a certain *Englischer* with raven black hair. A terribly handsome English boy."

"That is just gossip, of course," Katie said quickly. Afraid to lie and bring her past sins into the present, she added, "I'm happy to be among the Amish. This is where I belong."

"We all realize that, Katie." With a snap of a freshly starched napkin, Winnie closed her trap. "Since there's no one keeping you, and you're so happy and all, won't you please consider helping Jonathan and me, then? I've never had my chance for love, what with Sarah passing on at such a young age."

"The decision was never mine, it was my parents'."

40

Unperturbed, Winnie turned to her mother. "Okay, then. Mrs. Brenneman, will you and John please reconsider? The girls would be truly happy to have Katie's company, and her presence would solve a fair amount of problems for both Jonathan and me." She paused. "He has been working very hard at the lumber factory. It is a good job. He can't afford to miss any time off work."

"I am glad he is doing so well at the lumberyard. And I do understand that he can not take days off to tend to the girls."

Anna bit her lip and looked down when Katie tried to catch her eye.

Winnie seemed to take the moment as a good sign. "Please?"

"I'll talk to John," her mother finally said, breaking the silence. "Perhaps we can come to some agreement, after all."

Cheeks as rosy as a spring day, Winnie beamed. "*Danke.*" She turned to Katie. "And, thank you, too, Katie. There's no one else I would trust to care for the girls." Setting down the iron again, she said, "I'll write to Malcolm today and tell them that there is still hope."

"Nothing is decided, Winnie."

"But nothing is *not* decided, either." Moments later, Winnie Lundy left them, twenty napkins neatly pressed, but at least half that many more left to do.

Irritation sliced through Katie as she glared at the

chore. Surely the least she could have done was finish what she started! Oh, that was so like Winnie—determined and scatterbrained. More than one teacher had said it was a regrettable combination. "Well, now I must finish Winnie's chore."

"That girl doesn't give up, does she?" Anna said with a laugh. "I thought she was going to start digging her heels right through the wood floor."

Her mother chuckled. "She never was one to give up. Not even in a blue moon." Crossing the kitchen, her mother sneaked up behind Katie and gave her a squeeze. "I'll make everything all right, dear Daughter. Don't fret."

As always, her mother's touch made her feel better. "I won't."

"*Gut.* Now you two finish dinner preparations. I'm going to go check on things in the front parlor. This latest batch of visitors is a handful, I'll tell you that." She bustled out of the kitchen.

When they were alone, Anna looked at Katie with concern in her eyes. "Katie, are you okay?"

She did not feel okay at all. Instead she felt dizzy and flushed, like she'd been bent over too long picking beans from the garden. "*Jah.* Sure. Why?"

"Oh, I don't know. It just seems that you're not as happy as I thought you'd be." Softly, she said, "I thought you liked Jonathan."

"I do."

"Then why aren't you happier? You heard your mother. You're about to get what you want."

She was happy. But how could she admit all her insecurities to someone like Anna, who had experienced so much and now was just months away from marriage? "It's . . . it's just that Winnie and her bossy nature is vexing. We used to be such good friends." Picking up a dishcloth, she bent and swiped up a bit of flour that had fallen to the wooden floor. "I don't remember her always being so pushy. It's like she doesn't even want to listen to anyone but herself."

"She does sound desperate," Anna agreed. "But maybe it's just because she finally feels like it's her time for love and she's afraid to let the moment slip by." Moving across the kitchen to Katie's side, Anna picked up Katie's finished pie shell and carried it to the oven. "I bet she's still the same person you always knew underneath. Sometimes circumstances can change a person, you know?"

"I know."

Taking two bowls to the sink, Anna said, "Actually you are the one who sounds strange. Ever since I've known you, you've had an eye on Jonathan Lundy. Now, though, you seem far more wary of him. Did something happen between the two of you?"

"No. Nothing has ever happened." Or was ever likely to.

Of course, that was the problem. Longingly, Katie looked toward the door. Oh, how she wanted to get away from everyone, for just a little while.

"Well, then, are you embarrassed around Winnie? Do you think she knows about your feelings for her brother?"

"No," Katie said. She wished that Anna would just stop. *Stop.* Her feelings for Jonathan were too mixed up. Especially now.

"If you were embarrassed, I'd understand. It's hard admitting to having a fancy for someone's brother."

"I don't fancy him, Anna." The words came out harsher than she intended, but for the life of her, Katie wouldn't take them back. She was tired of being seen as only a silly girl. She was more than that. Why, if everyone only knew the things she'd done. . . .

They would be mighty surprised, for sure.

Eyes wide, Anna stepped back. "Sorry. I didn't mean to press."

Katie was sorry for her words, too. But she didn't feel like apologizing. Yet, she knew she must. "I'm the one who is sorry, Anna. Please forgive my sharp words."

Green eyes blinked. "Is there anything that I can help you with?"

"No."

"Is it me? Does my being here bother you?"

Finally she could speak the truth about something. "No, Anna. Your being here is wonderful *gut.* Truly. Now let's do what we're supposed to do, *jah*? We have to finish preparing dinner, cleaning the kitchen, and ironing napkins, just like *Maam* said."

Anna chuckled. "I'll finish up those napkins, Katie."

Later that day, after they'd served dinner, the kitchen had been cleaned and the animals tended to, after her father had read from the Bible and they all said good night, Katie was alone with only little Roman for company, snug in his basket with his favorite blanket that he liked to chew.

Carefully she opened the chest of drawers and pulled out a box from her past. A fancy papered box left from her time with the English. Like a fugitive, she'd smuggled it into the house, deathly afraid her mother would find it. Would ask why such a gaudy piece of work was in her possession.

Katie couldn't rightly say. All she did know was that she couldn't bear to part with the memories.

Not even the bad ones.

With a furtive glance toward the door, Katie carried the box to her bed and settled in. And then she lifted the lid. The heady fragrance of her secret life roared out of the enclosure like the spirit of Christmas past.

She blinked away the memories each scent envisioned.

Mint. A crushed rose. A tiny stuffed bear. Several fancy store-bought cards. With a sigh, Katie picked up the little brown bear and rubbed it

45

against her cheek. If she closed her eyes, she could remember receiving it. Remember the joy she'd felt. The longing for things that couldn't be.

Of things she shouldn't want.

As if burned, Katie hastily tucked it back into the box and closed it. But still the scent lingered. Remnants of another time. A time that unfortunately wasn't so long ago.

In her stark room, the memories seemed out of place. Foreign. As if they belonged to someone else. Someone reckless and wild. They belonged to the person she'd been for fifteen months.

It had all started out simply enough. She'd gone with two other teens to the back of Jonathan's land, where a duffel bag was hidden. Inside were jeans and sweaters and T-shirts. Donning them felt exciting and terribly scary.

She'd felt far more wicked when she took off her *kapp* and loosened her hair. Laura gave her an elastic to put it in a ponytail. Then she, Laura, and Laura's neighbor James walked to town.

Looking back, Katie knew they'd looked nothing like regular *Englischers*. She had the wide-eyed expression of a deer in the glade.

But when they'd gone into a coffee shop called the Brown Dog, Laura introduced Katie to Holly and her brother, Brandon. The moment Brandon had looked her way and suddenly smiled, Katie had been smitten.

Oh, he'd been so handsome. He'd looked just

like a man in one of Anna's fashion magazines that she'd shared with her back when she used to visit for quilting classes.

And Holly, well, she'd liked Holly so much, too. Though Holly was a few years older, she liked many of the things that Katie did. And she'd been so nice. So friendly. She introduced Katie, Laura, and James to a number of her friends. And because Holly had accepted her, the other teenagers had, too. One hour passed, then two. The next thing she knew, Laura was telling Katie that they needed to leave as soon as possible.

To her delight, Brandon had looked disappointed. "Can I have your phone number? I'll give you a call later."

Since of course the only phone they had was for business at the inn, she put him off. "My folks don't like me to receive phone calls."

"Oh. Well, how about I stop by?"

"No, that's probably not a good idea, either."

Puzzled, he raised his eyebrows. "Well, will you at least come back here soon?"

His eagerness to see her again brought forth a rush of pleasure. Had she ever felt so wanted before? "Sure. I can do that."

"Tomorrow? We'll be hanging out here again tomorrow."

Holly had grabbed her hand. "Please say you'll come back."

Though Laura and James were tapping their feet

impatiently at the front door, Katie nodded. "I will. I'll see you both tomorrow."

"Promise? We still have so much to talk about. You haven't even told me about your school or your friends."

"I will come back. I promise."

Moments later, Laura called out her name. "Katie, we must go *now*."

Holly chuckled as Katie practically ran out the door. "See you!"

The whole way home, Laura and James had talked about how strange the *Englischers* were. Laura in particular was uncomfortable. "If that is what we've been missing, I have to say I am glad," she'd stated. "Katie, did you see the way that one boy was looking at you? I think he liked you."

She had noticed. "I did."

"He talked to you a lot, too. What was he talkin' about?"

"Nothing special." The lie felt horrible sliding off her tongue, but Katie did her best to look innocent.

"He was fairly handsome, I mean for an English boy." With a sweet look toward James, Laura added, "I much prefer the Amish men I know."

Katie had said nothing, mainly because she'd known that Laura really only wanted James to notice her.

So, she never told a soul she had plans. Secret plans. The first of many.

Katie's hands shook as she stared at that box.

Quickly, she put it away, hoping its removal would banish the memories.

Still they remained, stark and vivid. Not the least bit faded.

Quickly she put on a thick nightgown, hoping the soft flannel would chase away the chill that was surrounding her.

After checking on Roman, who was still happily curled in a little ball, Katie crawled under the thick layers of blankets and quilts. But sleep wouldn't come. Why was she thinking about Holly and Brandon after all this time?

Could it be because of the things that Brandon had said? Because lately she was realizing that maybe no one would ever say words like that to her again?

Katie closed her eyes to ward off the memory. To ward off the wishes.

When no relief came, she did the only thing she could—she prayed to the only one who could give her peace. "God, please help me. I've been so good lately. I'm doing everything I can to make amends. Is that what is important? Is that enough?"

Only silence met her words. Swallowing hard, she spoke a little louder. "Lord, I can't go back to the way I was. I need the protection of my family, of my Order. I need Your healing grace. Please stay with me and hold me. Walk by my side. Show me the way." She closed her eyes and prayed one of her favorite verses. "Blessed is everyone who fears the

Lord, who walks in his ways." But even the quote from Psalm 128 did little to ease her burdens.

In fact, all Katie noticed was that the lingering scent of roses and mint still hung thick in the air.

Katie was playing with Roman, enjoying the rare afternoon sun when Henry approached, his expression as serious as if he was going to a burial.

"Someone left this for you at McClusky General Store," Henry said as he handed her a white business-sized envelope.

As she turned it over in her hands, worry gripped her. "Did *Daed* see it?"

"No." He looked at her curiously. "The person said it was for an Amish girl named Katie. Ron said he didna know of anyone else by that name. Is it yours?"

"Maybe. Probably." As she looked at the writing on the envelope, Katie fought to keep her expression innocent.

It was mighty hard to do, because from the moment she'd spied the writing on the envelope, she'd known immediately that the letter was for her and her alone. More important, she also knew who the author was. Holly's handwriting had had those distinctive curves. No one else had ever written her name so fancy.

It seemed a strange coincidence that Holly had written her so soon after she'd just been thinking about her.

Unfortunately, Henry was not as easy to fool as she might have hoped. "Katie, who would be writing you in care of the general store? What is the note about?"

"Nothing. I . . . made some friends among the English. You know that. This must be from one of them."

"But you aren't looking at the note like it's from a dear friend. You are looking at it like it might bite you."

She gripped it harder. Wished she could just wish it away. Wish that neither Henry nor she had ever seen it. With even greater effort, Katie fought to keep her voice calm and neutral. "Don't be silly."

Still playing detective, Henry said, "If this person is such a good friend, why didn't she have your address? Why all the secrecy?"

"I don't know the answer. I haven't opened the letter yet, have I?"

"Well, then, open it up." He crossed his arms over his chest and waited, just like he'd used to do when they'd walk to school and she hadn't been able to keep up with his long stride.

There was no way she wanted him to spy the contents. She slipped it in the pocket of her apron. "I will, later."

"But—"

"It's private, Henry."

"Private?" A pair of lines formed between his brows.

In her pocket, the letter's weight burned. "I'm allowed privacy too, aren't I?" Remembering how she'd interrupted him and Anna kissing just two days ago, she said, "Or is privacy only for courting couples?"

Henry bowed his head in embarrassment. "Of course you may have your privacy. You are as prickly as a cactus lately. I don't know what's wrong with you."

"Nothing is wrong, Henry."

"You canna fool me, Sister. I've known you too long for that."

After securing Roman in one of the stalls in the barn, Katie scrambled to her room, letter safely hidden in her apron, Henry's words echoing in her heart.

Yes, she had changed. And it didn't matter how sweet and kind she tried to be now. Inside, where it counted, she'd always be the girl who made a very big mistake . . . and had run from it.

As she stared at the letter she only knew one thing for certain: she was wanted again.

Chapter 4

Winnie was in good spirits. "Malcolm's letter was a full three pages. He gave me news about his family and their neighbors. He sends his good wishes to you, Jonathan."

"I appreciate that," Jonathan mumbled. When

Winnie looked up, he turned back to his task of loading the wagon so she wouldn't see his expression. It was getting harder and harder to keep his personal feelings about Winnie's pen pal to himself. It was even more difficult to refrain from sharing his thoughts about her infatuation.

"Do you appreciate his wishes? You don't sound like you do." She walked by his side as he continued to load the wagon. Halfheartedly, she shoved in a pail of nails next to a pile of wood. "You don't sound interested in my letter at all."

The moment she turned, Jonathan rearranged things so the nails wouldn't fall over.

"This letter, it is your business, not mine." When he noticed her shoulders slump, he wished he could take back his words. But really, at the moment, he begrudged his sister's interest in Malcolm Troyer. He was an interloper in their life.

"Well, he extended an invitation again."

"Uh-huh." Jah, this Malcolm was an inconvenience, that's what he was. He needed Winnie's attention here in Ohio. Jonathan needed her help with the girls.

Plus, he had no desire to stand around and discuss every written word in Winnie's letters yet again. His sister could wrestle with each sentence's meaning for an hour at a time.

He had no desire to do that. Besides, he'd been meaning to work the back fences today. There was much to do, since he only had Saturdays to get anything done. Over the last few years, he'd gradually worked more at the lumberyard with Brent and farmed less. The money was better, and far more stable. That was a good thing, since so much in his personal life felt unsteady.

Still holding the letter, Winnie said, "It's time I went to visit him. Past time."

"It's a shame he can't travel here. That's the way of things, don't you agree?"

"I already told you that his father is sick, and that Malcolm must run their hardware store. Honestly, Jonathan, didn't you hear me?"

"I heard you." Yes, he heard her, but other things weighed on his mind, most especially Mary and Hannah. Once again, they'd seemed whiny and angry the evening before. Mary had gone about her chores so slowly that they took double the time that they should. Hannah just frowned and clutched the doll Sarah had made for her even tighter.

It's been almost two years now, Lord. When are You going to make things better?

"Jonathan?"

"I'm sorry. I am, *uh,* interested, just busy, you know."

She took his apology without much thought. "I worry about planning ahead, but I feel that something is mighty special between me and Malcolm." Dimples showing, she blurted, "For the first time in my life, I have hope for a family of my own. Perhaps I'll be planning a wedding soon."

54

Jonathan bent down to pick up a shovel in order to hide his scowl. Winnie sounded so happy and optimistic. However, at the moment, he couldn't think of a worse thing than Winnie courting and marrying. What would he do with the girls then?

"Jonathan?" She picked up the leather glove he dropped. "What do you think?"

With a nod of thanks, he took the glove and paired it with the other. "I think you're counting chickens," he mumbled, though even to his own ears he knew he sounded grumpy and terribly old. When had he forgotten what it was like to be in love? To want to be in love?

"Not necessarily."

"Winnie, you've never even met this man, face-to-face."

"But I will soon."

"Well, I just don't want you to go getting your hopes up." Now that was a foolish thing to say, indeed! Her hopes were already up so high, a kite could be attached to them.

"Did you and Sarah always know you were going to be married?"

The question brought to mind images of Sarah. Of her ruddy face and matter-of-fact ways. Of her easy laugh. Of the first time he'd kissed her. "No. Not always."

"When, then?"

"I couldn't say." When had he first thought about a life with Sarah? When he'd first spied her at a neighbor's wedding? When he'd known she'd return his feelings?

Winnie leaned against the wagon. "Come now, Brother. Tell me something worth remembering."

"There isn't much to tell." And there really wasn't. If a person was looking for a story about flowers and romance, their engagement was surely not it.

But because Winnie still waited for a reply, and she did so much for him, and because she was asking and she didn't ask for much, he tried to remember. Slowly Jonathan said, "As you know, Sarah and I met when we were young. Courting and marriage seemed like a *gut* idea."

"You were anxious, right? You married young."

Had he been anxious? All he remembered was that it had been expected and he had no reason not to marry Sarah. But that sounded so harsh. Clearing his throat, he murmured, "We were ready. *Mamm* and *Daed* helped us, remember? We lived at home for quite a time."

All moony eyed, Winnie nodded. "I remember that. You and Sarah, down the hall."

Yes. To his shame, Jonathan had been terribly happy with the arrangement. His mother had been a good buffer between him and his demanding, outspoken bride who always had something to say about everyone and everything. At least once a day he would wish she'd hold her tongue more. But she never did.

No, Sarah was a gregarious sort. That was for sure. She'd always eagerly invited scores of people over to their home, creating extra work for everyone. She had often complained about how much he worked and finally asked him to spend most of Saturdays with her. She'd never understood his need to work.

She'd never understood his reluctance to be around people. No, Sarah had not been a wallflower. Not even a little bit of one.

Winnie cleared her throat. "Jonathan? Well? What happened then?"

"You know what happened. We moved here. Then . . . well, you know . . ."

"Everything's so different now." A cloud fell over his sister's face.

That much was true. Not two years after he and Sarah had taken their vows, their father was diagnosed with cancer and died. Then Sarah's accident . . . What would have happened if Sarah had not been so intent to return from her outing at twilight, on such a foggy night? The dim light, combined with the fog, had made it near impossible for the approaching car to see either the reflective tape on the side or the slow-moving vehicle sign on the back of the buggy. Within seconds, Sarah was severely injured, the buggy mere toothpicks, and the horse dead. Sarah had died before the ambulance reached the hospital.

After the accident, when he and his girls were

still numb, his mother had lived with him. Last year, when it became obvious her health was failing, too, she announced that she would go live with her sister, his aunt up near Lancaster, Pennsylvania. It was decided that Winnie would be a better helpmate to Jonathan and the girls.

"Our family has had its share of sadness," he said, though that statement didn't near describe all the topsy-turvy turns his life had taken.

Winnie pushed away from the side of the wagon and practically skipped by his side. "I'm fair to bursting about going to Indiana. I hope Katie comes to her senses soon."

Oh, how uncomfortable that visit to the Brennemans had been. He'd near ripped his hat in two, he'd been gripping it so hard. "I hope so, too."

"I have a feeling that something else is going on besides Irene and John not wanting her near you. Did you get that feeling, too?"

"It doesna matter what I think."

"Now Katie is someone who I'm surprised didn't marry right away. She's so pretty. When we were best friends, all she ever talked about was wanting to be in love. I tell you, I always saw her making little things for her hope chest and planning her marriage. What do you think happened? Why do you think she hasn't met her match?"

He walked to the barn to get Blacky, their horse. "Don't ask me about such things."

"Don't be such a stick in the mud. Come now, you must have had some thoughts on her."

Katie Brenneman was a fair sight, for sure. Blue eyes as fresh as spring. A slim, becoming figure. Light brown hair always plaited neatly under her *kapp*. A pleasant disposition. A pretty smile and an adorable way about her that had always drawn him close. "Her married state is none of our business."

"I know, but—"

"I best get going, Winnie. You know I canna stop and chat all day. Work has to get done."

"Oh, all right. Jonathan, you are far too serious sometimes."

"I know." He kept walking in silence, but privately argued fiercely over that. When he was younger, he'd been always up for fun and mischief. He loved a good joke, either of the practical nature or a simple story.

Time and again, their father had encouraged him to mind his manners a bit more. Sarah, on the other hand, had wanted him to be more lighthearted all the time.

Yes, Sarah had never had a problem with telling him what she thought.

Jonathan had a feeling life with Katie would be different. She had a sweet way about her and an easy laugh. Yes, he did, indeed, find her very pleasing. He'd also been aware that she'd fancied him. And though he shouldn't feel flattered and full of himself, he did, indeed.

We need to talk about Brandon. Can you meet me on Sunday at noon? I'll be at the Brown Dog Café, just like old times.

Katie's hands shook as she stared at the note again. What would it be like, going back to the Brown Dog? She hadn't been there since she'd confessed everything to Brandon and Holly. She'd certainly never stepped inside the coffeehouse dressed Amish.

Church services at neighbors' homes only took place every other Sunday. This Sunday was an off week, so she'd be able to go, if she really wanted to.

The Brown Dog was in walking distance, if a person didn't mind the windy roads to get there. Situated in Peebles, it sat on the outskirts of a small town and attracted a variety of people. Mostly teenagers and college students hung out in the booths and old tables. Mixed in with the teenagers were a few young adults eager to take a break. Katie had liked the place from the moment she'd followed James and Laura inside.

The walls were exposed red brick. Black-and-white photos in silver frames hung scattered all over the walls. The scenes were of places in Europe. Exotic places Katie had never dreamed of seeing.

Places Katie knew she'd most likely never visit.

And that had bothered her mightily when she was seventeen. She'd opened her eyes to music and art and fashion and had been inundated with sites and smells and images so completely unfamiliar and strange that she'd been drawn to them.

Not so her other Amish friends. No, Laura and James had first taken her there one evening, but then had found nothing in the Brown Dog that was worthy of note. After that, Katie had gone by herself.

Events had spiraled at a breakneck speed, then fell apart, shattered as a finely made glass. The shards had pricked her, too. Some still lay embedded in her skin, pushing to get out, making her wince if she moved suddenly. If she forgot they were there.

When she'd left Brandon and Holly for the very last time, Katie had felt terribly embarrassed and ashamed. It had been difficult to admit to being a liar for almost two years. And that was what she had been.

Their questions and confusion had echoed in Katie's mind long after she'd torn out the front door, grabbed her bicycle, and pedaled as quickly as she dared back to everything that was familiar. Right then and there, she'd promised herself to never stray again from the Amish way of life. To never pretend to be someone she wasn't.

An hour later, in the woods bordering the Lundys' farm, Katie hopped off the bicycle, removed the jeans and sweater, and slipped back on her dress. The air had been chilly—she'd welcomed the sting on her skin. With easy, comforting movements, she'd braided her hair and positioned her *kapp*. By dipping a cloth into the edge of the river, she'd removed the last sheen of pink lip gloss.

Finally, she gathered up all her "English" clothes into a pillowcase and tossed them into the river. After valiantly attempting to float, the items sunk.

Very slowly, she walked the rest of the way home. Head down. Proper. Circumspect. But she couldn't forget who she'd pretended to be.

We need to talk.

Stunned into the present again, Katie stared at the words. The note sounded so desperate and sure. What in the world could Holly want? What could she possibly want to speak to Katie about after all this time?

More important, what had happened in Holly's life to prod her to even want to contact Katie? Holly had been so mad when Katie had confessed everything. Katie would've thought nothing would ever have encouraged Holly to seek her out. The note sounded urgent and determined, which made Katie feel even more on edge.

Closing her eyes, Katie remembered so many good times she'd shared with Holly and Brandon. They'd gone to the mall, hung out in front of the TV, all things that Katie knew weren't wrong. But the web of lies she'd told about her life at home had been.

She'd made up stories about super-strict parents

and baby sisters so Holly and Brandon would stop asking to visit her house. She'd held Brandon's hand and let him speak to her about proms and dances and college visits—just as if she would one day do all those things.

With a rush of heat, she remembered the feel of Brandon's arms around her, the way his lips had felt against her own when they'd kissed for the first time. The way he'd looked at her, like he really liked her. Like she was special.

Her parents thought they knew most of what she'd done. That was why they'd been so confused about her decision to join the church as quickly as possible. But they didn't know everything.

They couldn't.

If they did, they'd never look at her the same, and Katie wouldn't be able to hold her head up in their community. Good people didn't do the things she'd done. Most important, good Christians didn't tell lie after lie to people who cared about them.

Did they?

Despair filtered through her once again. How could this all have happened, anyway? She'd prayed to God to help her move on with her life. Why hadn't He listened? Why had He encouraged Holly to contact her?

Katie wanted to tear up the paper. She wanted to burn it and turn it to ashes. To pretend it had never arrived.

That is what she would do. It was her only

option. She couldn't visit the Brown Dog now, even if she'd been inclined. She was no longer a dreamy girl who was a tad bit rebellious. She was a responsible woman now. Moreover, there was a chance she was finally about to get to know Jonathan better. That couldn't be ignored.

But what would happen if she didn't go? Most likely nothing. Holly might be angry, but she surely wouldn't care if she never saw Katie again. Yes, that was the right thing to do. Keep the past in the past, where it belonged. Where she wouldn't have to think about it.

Where she could pretend it had never really happened.

"Katie, there you are, Daughter."

With a start, Katie noticed her mother standing in her doorway. She scrambled to a sitting position. "*Mamm.*"

"Haven't you heard me? I've been calling for you time and again."

"I'm sorry." After stuffing the letter and envelope under a pillow behind her, Katie stood up. "What do you need?"

"Your time, of course." After treating Katie to a particularly pointed glare, her mother turned on her heel and headed downstairs.

Katie had no choice but to follow. Her steps sounded louder than usual as they clopped on the wooden stairs, the noise jarring the relative peace of the inn.

After a burst of guests, their inn was remarkably quiet. Just the other day, Henry had announced that there'd been a curious drop in reservations for the next two weeks. The news was unusual, but not unwelcome, at least to her brother.

Katie knew Henry would rather work on projects in the workshop or fuss over Anna. He might call it "tutoring," but he was as besotted as any man in love and didn't try hard to hide it.

After entering the hearth room in silence, Irene Brenneman sat on the couch next to her husband. Roman had followed. Now he was there, too, sprawled out on the braided rug and chewing on a knotted piece of rope Henry had fashioned for him.

After gently scratching Roman's ears, Katie moved to sit across from her parents. Her heart was beating so loud, Katie was sure her parents could hear it.

Without fanfare, her mother said, "Your father and I've been talking about Jonathan and his offer for you."

"Oh." Katie swallowed with relief. Oh, for a moment she'd been sure they were going to question her about the letter.

Her father's lips twitched. "That is not the response I had imagined you would have."

Katie thought quickly. "I don't have any response prepared. I assumed a decision had been made."

"It had not." After glancing her father's way, her

mother replied. "After Winnie came by and we had that discussion, your father and I did some more thinking. In a nutshell, Katie, we have reconsidered."

Their decision caught her off guard. "I'm surprised. I didn't think you wanted me to be at the Lundy home."

"In truth, we do not."

"Then why are you allowing me to go? What has changed your mind?"

With a weary expression, her father pulled out his knife and picked up the latest cane he was working on, obviously needing something to occupy his hands. After carefully lifting off a layer of birch, he met her eyes. "While it is true we did not want you to live at the Lundys', we decided that perhaps we were not right in withholding this opportunity because of our reasons."

"I'm not sure what reasons you mean."

Her mother sighed. "Daughter, simply put, we know you have particular feelings for Jonathan. We do not want to see you get hurt." Her mother's eyes turned worried as she continued. "Jonathan may not ever care about you the way you might wish. He might not ever want to marry again."

It was mortifying to know that her feelings for Jonathan were so obvious. "I know that."

"And you are fine with that? In two months' time, you could return here without a hint of a future with Jonathan."

That was most likely true. But no matter what, Katie couldn't deny that she wanted to be near him. She also wanted him to get a chance to see her in a whole new way: as Katie; as a capable, considerate woman, not just as Henry's little sister. "I'm fine with the risk. No matter what, I think it will be an adventure for me."

Her father scowled. "A mighty strange adventure, I think."

"In many ways, you are still an impulsive girl, Katie," her mother said slowly. "I had hoped that in time you would have learned to curb it."

"I have."

"Have you? Truly?" Her father glided the knife over the wood with ease. Under his hand, a smooth sphere was taking shape. "We know you did some things of which you might not feel proud. Back when you were younger."

The world felt like it was spinning too fast. Was this about the letter, after all?

Had Henry already somehow read her letter? Had he also blabbed to Anna and her parents about the contents? "Those times are behind me."

"Time can not always be forgotten, Katie. It passes, but our deeds stay with us. Mark us. For good or bad, our past transgressions and deeds make us who we are—even when we do things just to see what they are like. Even when we do things without meaning to hurt ourselves or other people."

Her father's words were true. She did feel marked and jaded. "I have tried to continue on the best that I could. I think I have been successful."

"We know that."

"Do you?" Thinking about how time and again she'd been asked to tutor Anna, Katie blurted, "You have asked my help for Anna. I have tried my best to teach her much about our life. You seem to trust me to teach her well. But when it comes to trusting me to make good decisions, you act as if I am too young. I am not too young."

"That is true. And it is also true that you have been a fine teacher for Anna, and an able helper at the inn," her mother said. "Your actions have shown us your sincerity time and again."

Her father smiled gently. "It is with that in mind that we've been reluctant to see you go from us. But that is not the right thing, I don't believe. Everyone needs to follow their own path, even if it isn't quite what parents always want."

"Yes, my Katie. It is time we let you go."

Her mother sounded resigned. With some surprise, Katie realized this time was as difficult for her parents as it was for her. They loved her.

Katie realized one day she, too, would marry, have children, and then eventually let them go. For the first time, she was able to acknowledge her parents' struggle—of letting her make decisions, even when they might be different from the ones they would have chosen. "Following God's path is not always an easy one to take," Katie murmured. "Sometimes I don't always know what He wants me to do."

"That is why there are rules to our society, the Ordnung. That is why He gave you family and friends, to lovingly guide you. Remember, Katie, no matter what, you are never alone."

Katie blinked. While her father's words now felt comforting, there'd also been a time when they'd sounded mighty confining, as well. "Yes, *Daed*. I . . . I don't want to be alone."

More gently, her mother murmured, "Of course not. Take care now, Katie. No one asks for perfection. We are all flawed."

"Sometimes, it is hard to see everyone else's flaws. I only seem to see my own."

"Then look around you more carefully. Look at Anna and her struggles."

Katie couldn't help but chuckle. Anna's attempts to become one of them had not been without amusements. Anna's canning mishaps were becoming legendary. When she wasn't burning her fingers on hot jam, she was struggling over the water baths for the jars. But still, she'd overcome many things. "I would never have guessed Henry would be so patient with her."

Her mother wasn't laughing. Instead, she pushed the conversation deeper once again. "Henry, he cares for Anna. He knows she has made mistakes, but he also has forgiven her, and seen that those mistakes made her stronger."

Katie had never heard her mother speak that way. In the past, it had always seemed that her parents had expected only obedience and perfection. Anything less was treated as a disappointment. That had been hard when she'd been following Rebekeh's footsteps. Her older sister—a full six years older than herself—had made everyone so proud, so seemingly effortlessly, Katie had always known that she'd never measure up.

When Katie's silence continued, her mother leaned forward. "Anna feels the same way."

"I know."

"She's made a fair amount of sacrifices for her love. She's given up so much."

Katie looked at her mother in surprise. "I never think of you ever seeing the outside world as something to give up."

"Why is that? Katie, though you seem hard-pressed to forget such things, I, too, was once much younger. I know of the distractions and the temptations that can entice us all. Yet you and I only had a few years of the outside world. Until Anna came here, it was truly all she'd ever known. That is a very big sacrifice, I think."

To her shame, Katie realized she had begun to take Anna's efforts for granted.

"But are you sure you want to help at the Lundys'?" her *mamm* asked. "I fear it will be a thankless task."

At least Katie knew she was not hoping for heaps

of praise at the Lundys'. "I am not looking for thanks." Steadfastly, she told herself that she was not looking for affection from Jonathan, either.

"Mary is a difficult child."

Mary was still hurting from the loss of her mother. "I think I may be able to help. And I do want to help them. Even Winnie." Winnie, who also was searching for the right helpmate in life.

"Yes, I can see that." But still *Mamm*'s voice sounded doubtful.

Wondering the cause, Katie said, "Do you think Winnie has found her true love? Or do you think she's just following a flight of fancy?"

Her mother's eyes opened wide. "I don't know. Dreams are all fair and good, and have their place in our lives. And as for true love—why, it's a fanciful thing, I think. Love comes after a time of working side by side and believing in each other. But I do have to admit that I think it is not unreasonable for her to want to follow her own heart for a change. She should not be expected to always feel content to raise her brother's children. Winnie has always wanted a family of her own."

"Love, side by side. Was that how love was with you and *Daed*?"

To Katie's amazement, her parents shared a warm smile. "I don't know how our hearts became joined. Your father and I felt love and companionship. He made me feel peaceful and whole."

Katie thought of Jonathan. Thought of how her

71

heart jumped whenever he was near. Truly, she never felt "peace" in his presence. No, it was more like a jumpy, nervous pounding in her heart, where every sense was on alert. Was that how she was supposed to feel? Or was there something different between them? Something more fanciful and dreamy? Fake.

Patting Katie's hand, her mother murmured, "Please pray on this, Katie. Take out what everyone else wants, and pray on the Lord's guidance. Then you'll know."

"I'll know." Her smile was brave. Inside, though, she was breaking.

Katie feared she'd never know what God wished her to do. Would never know what the Lord wanted.

Or worse, Katie feared that she would be unable to do what He asked. Deep dread filled her once again. If she couldn't carry out the Lord's will, what would she do then?

More important, what kind of person would she be then?

Chapter 5

"Henry, I just don't know if I'll ever be as good an Amish wife as you deserve," Anna Metzger said as she entered his workshop in the barn.

He chuckled but didn't look up from the bridle he was oiling. "Anna, the things you say. What brought this on?"

"Oh, I don't know." It had been a particularly trying day. It was bitterly cold, she was tired, and in a burst of selfish temper, she had told Katie that she wished she were back home, tucked in an electric blanket, watching TV.

Needless to say, that remark hadn't gone over very well.

But she couldn't share that with Henry, so she just shrugged, her eyes still on him, willing him to look up and say something to make her feel better.

Instead of talking, he held out a hand. The gesture was perfect, so Henrylike. Eager for a reassuring hug, she approached, but somehow managed to trip over one of Roman's toys. Henry reached for her just as she'd held out her hands to stop her fall. "Anna, are you all right?"

Her ankle did throb, but not enough to complain about. Unfortunately, though, tears still threatened to spill. It had been that kind of day. "I'm fine. Just embarrassed."

After settling her in his seat, Henry stood up and rubbed her shoulders. For a second, Anna thought he was going to cuddle her close. But, like always, his inner resolve and obedience shone through. Instead, he leaned forward, looked into her eyes, and gently smoothed back a lock of her blond hair into the confines of her *kapp*. When he spied her tears, he murmured, "Do you have a headache, *liewe* Anna?"

Liewe Anna. *Dear* Anna. A little flutter raced

across her heart at the sweet words. Since he knew about her occasional migraines, she sought to put him at ease. "No. It's just been a long day."

Stepping a few inches away, he took her hands. "What happened?"

"Everything and nothing. I messed up a few things and spoke harshly to Katie. And, well, I hadn't seen you in hours."

Dawning understanding lit his eyes, along with a fair amount of humor. "I see."

Oops. Henry really did see. She'd come in for his attention, which she missed very much. It was hard to find time alone with him, even though they were almost a courting couple.

And though Katie warned her that it was not the Amish way to speak of such things, Anna knew that she longed to be in Henry's arms and perhaps steal a kiss or two. Before she could stop herself, she laid her head on his shoulder. Instead of moving away, Henry curved his arms around her back. "I've missed you too, Anna," he murmured, pressing his lips to her temple.

If Anna didn't know better, she would have guessed that Henry was very wise in the ways of the world. Very wise in relationships and the silliness and insecurities of women. That was disconcerting. But at the moment, it was comforting, too. After hugging him tightly, she pulled away. It wouldn't do for his father to come in and see them hugging. "I guess I should go now."

"Because?"

"I don't want to disturb you."

"You are not disturbing me." *Ah,* but a shadow fell away from his eyes. Something bright and playful took its place. Perhaps he wasn't immune to her, either? "Did you have another bout with the laundry?"

Anna was sure she would never like doing laundry. She hadn't even liked washing clothes when she'd had every modern convenience at her disposal. Now doing much of it by hand was particularly difficult. She'd found pinning garments to clotheslines especially challenging—at least once a week a pair of pants, a dress, or a quilt would fly off the line, get soiled, and need to be washed again. "No. I just seem to do something wrong every day." She pointed to her ankle. "I mean, come on, who else trips over dog toys and stumbles in her skirts?"

Eyes sparkling, he murmured, "You are not the first person to trip." With an amused expression, he glanced down at Roman, who was inspecting a spider in the corner of the room. "And puppies do have a lot of toys."

"I know, but it's just so silly."

"No one is judging you, Anna. Truth be told, everyone is in awe of your efforts."

"Even you?" She didn't want him to regret choosing her.

Heat replaced mischief in his expression. "Especially me," he murmured.

To her delight, he reached for both of her hands once again and linked his fingers through hers. "Most especially me."

"I just hope you know what you are getting. I'm not perfect. And what's more, I don't think I ever will be perfect."

Gently, surprisingly, he rubbed the tops of her knuckles with his thumb. Though slightly calloused, it felt warm and sent yet another spark of awareness through her. And another jolt of longing for him. "Hush, now. I don't want perfection, I want you. What's more, I never forget the sacrifices you are making for me. It is not an easy way of life, ours."

"I don't mind. This is the place for me."

"I am grateful for that. But, what about you?"

"What do you mean?"

A knowing look entered his eyes. "You're getting the same old Henry. Perhaps you are disappointed?"

"Never. I could never be disappointed with you."

Anna glimpsed a hint of satisfaction, completely male and especially tender, enter his eyes before she closed her own, just as he kissed her.

When they parted, Anna couldn't resist pressing her fingers to her lips. "Oh."

"You are not alone, Anna. I promise, you are not alone."

She didn't know if his words or his actions flustered her more. "I . . . I better go work on the laundry again. The clothespins don't always stay . . ."

"I'll see you at supper."

"Yes." And then she ran. Maybe everything was going to be just fine, after all.

"And, Katie, this is where you will sleep," Winnie finished, pointing to a bare guest room. Only a twin bed with a dark pair of quilts, a forlorn bedside table with an ancient-looking kerosene lamp, and a thick shade decorated the room. Though the November sun was shining merrily outside, no one inside of this guest room would ever guess that such a thing was happening. It was as dark and gloomy as if the sun never peeked out among the clouds.

"I don't see hooks for clothes. Are there any?"

"Oh yes, I forgot. Jonathan said he would bring in a chest of drawers from the *daadi haus* and nail up some hooks soon."

It was a most unpleasant, bare, and cold space, devoid of even a bright quilt to warm things. Everything looked cold and stark—so different from the guest rooms at the inn.

At their inn, each room had been given particular care and attention. Framed quilts adorned the walls, while a pleasing mix of traditional quilts and thick goose-down comforters covered the beds. Fluffy feather pillows and thick, crisp sheets made each bed a welcoming sight after a day of sightseeing or hard work. And the rooms smelled different—like lemon oil and sunshine.

This room smelled musty and worn, as if it hadn't been opened or aired out in years. Surely that couldn't be the truth? "Did you empty it for me and my things?"

Winnie blinked. "No, it's never been used all that much. It's just an extra place to sleep, after all."

"Back at the inn—"

"Neither Jonathan nor I have had the time or intention to worry about decorating a bedroom." Softening, she added, "I'm sorry, Katie. I know it's not what you're used to."

Now Katie felt ashamed, indeed, of worrying about such vanities. "It's fine."

As Winnie scanned the room again, she frowned, regret in her gaze. "I suppose things do look a bit gloomy. You are more than welcome to spruce things up to suit you."

"You wouldn't mind?"

"Not at all. Jonathan and I want you to be happy here."

But Katie heard every word that was unspoken, clear as day. Winnie was saying if Katie thought a cozy, pretty bedroom was important, then she was spending her time focusing on the wrong things.

"This room is . . . fine."

As if looking at the room for the first time, Winnie scrunched up her brow. "Your inn is a beautiful place, to be sure."

"It's fine," she said again. Yes, the inn was beautiful, but Katie was very aware of the amount of time she'd spent polishing spindles, starching and ironing curtains, washing walls, and waxing floors. "I didn't come here to have fancy knickknacks."

"Oh. Yes." Winnie swallowed. "I know you came to help us out. To help me, most especially. I am grateful."

"You are most welcome. I had a need to come here, as well."

As if reading Katie's mind, Winnie murmured, "I'm sorry Jonathan wasn't here. His boss couldn't let him off today. He mentioned something about a big order for a builder in Michigan."

Obviously, everyone knew about her infatuation with Jonathan! "There's no need to apologize. I didn't expect him to be here, waiting for me."

"But I am sure it would have been nice. After all, this is his home."

"Don't worry so, Winnie. You've got a suitcase to pack and a trip to get ready for."

Winnie's cheeks bloomed bright. "I can't believe that tomorrow I'll be boarding a bus to Indianapolis! I'm *naerfich*—as nervous as a young schoolgirl."

Katie could scarce believe it, either. From the moment she'd made her decision, with God's help, to go live at the Lundy home, things had moved with lightning speed. Now, here it was, the second week in November, and she was moving into her new room.

Yes, she'd been as busy as a bee during the last

two days. At the inn, Anna helped her pack and asked a dozen questions about completing some of the chores Katie usually did. Her *mamm* and *daed* had each pulled her aside and offered bits of encouragement and advice.

Even Henry had offered her a hand and had promised to take care of the pup in her absence. Katie had been grateful for her family's support, realizing once again how strong their love was. They were willing to support her and help even when they didn't completely agree with her actions.

Thinking again of Holly's letter, Katie wondered what everyone would say if they met Holly or Brandon. Most likely, everyone would like them a lot. It would only be when people realized how close Katie had been to loving Brandon and to leaving the community that eyebrows would be raised.

Of course, she wouldn't have to guess what her sister, Rebekeh, would have to say about lying to them. Rebekeh would be critical, indeed. "It's a shame you haven't yet put into practice the teachings of the Bible, Katie," she would say. "Perhaps you should do some more thinking and praying about treating others with care and concern."

Then Katie would feel exactly how she always did around her sister—childish and inept. Because it had been Katie in the wrong.

Not Holly. Certainly not Brandon.

After closing her new bedroom door behind them, Katie and Winnie walked down the scuffed oak planks that lined the hall. The walls were painted a glossy white but were as bare and plain as most of the other walls in the home. As Winnie pointed out a few drawings that Mary did, and they joked about the art projects they'd once done side by side, Katie felt herself warming to Winnie once again. Eager to return to their former easy camaraderie. "I would also be terribly nervous about going all the way to Indiana, Winnie. It is hard to travel by oneself."

"I've scarcely thought about the travel. I can only think about meeting Malcolm for the first time." Picking up an envelope from the kitchen table, Winnie murmured, "I just know he's going to be as perfect as I've dreamed him to be."

"But what if he is not? Win, what if you find you don't like Malcolm? Then what will you do?"

"I . . . I don't know. I've never considered such a thing, to be honest. The letters we've shared are wonderful. No man who writes such words could be much different in person."

Katie knew better. She knew firsthand how people could look one way but be far different inside. She'd been that way for a time.

She and Winnie spent the majority of the day working side by side. Winnie had carefully written out the girls' usual routine and had shown Katie where to find everything necessary for cleaning and cooking. They walked the large cellar where only a few fruits and vegetables had been canned.

Katie bit her tongue rather than ask what in the world Winnie had been doing. Amish women were proud of their home and took great pains to see that it was pleasing to the eye and a comfortable haven for all. After all, the home was the heart of the family.

In addition, most women busily canned from sunup to sunset several times a week at harvest time, carefully storing food for the winter and spring. If the job was too big for a woman to do on her own, neighbors and relatives were only too happy to help. Katie had accompanied her mother on many an occasion to help can or freeze necessities for the coming year.

But, now that she thought of it, Katie couldn't think of a time during their long friendship when Winnie had ever asked for help. She'd always tried to be self-sufficient as possible.

Maybe she should have offered to help Winnie more?

Katie noticed that there was little mention of Jonathan in Winnie's notes. Because she wanted to please him, she said, "What about Jonathan? You've got nothing written about his needs. What time does he leave for work? When does he return? What do you make for his lunch?"

Winnie frowned. "He's a grown man, Katie. He can take care of himself."

That sounded surprising to Katie. All Amish women took pride in taking care of their families. Did Winnie never attempt to help Jonathan with his meals?

She was prevented from saying anything more by the arrival of Mary and Hannah. "Hello, girls," she said with a smile as she hurriedly tried to help them off with their cloaks and hang them on the hooks by the back door. "I've been eager all day to see you both."

Seven-year-old Mary stopped in her tracks. "Katie, you're here already?"

Winnie clucked. "Remember how I told you this morning that Katie would be comin' to stay today?"

Wordlessly, Mary grasped Hannah's hand. They both nodded.

Katie looked to Winnie with a smile. "I'll be here for two months. Are you two ready to help me?"

Mary looked at Hannah, then at Katie with a reproachful glare. "No." She then walked away, leaving her lunch pail and satchel on the table.

Katie waited for Winnie to chastise the girl. But instead of correcting the girl's behavior, Winnie merely picked up Mary's abandoned items and put them to rights.

Yet more strange behavior followed. Dinner was a haphazard affair. No one waited for Jonathan. Instead, Winnie just put some food on a plate for him.

After dinner, the girls went up to their room instead of gathering around the hearth like Katie's family always did. Soon after, Winnie went to her room to finish packing.

Finally, at almost seven o'clock, Jonathan entered. As soon as he noticed her presence, his steps slowed. "Katie. You came."

"Of course I did. I said I would." When she smiled his way, Jonathan blinked and he dipped his chin, as if embarrassed.

"Well, I'm . . . glad. The girls need you here." He looked at her again, then turned away.

"I had a busy day. Winnie showed me around your home."

"I hope you found everything to your liking."

Suddenly, she couldn't have cared less about her bare room or the unfamiliar surroundings. "Everything is most pleasing."

After removing his black coat and hanging his hat on a peg by the door, he walked quickly to the sink, washed his hands, then picked up the plate she'd set out for him. "Is this for me?"

"Of course." Taking a chance, she dared to tease him a bit. "Who else would it be for? I hope you like meat loaf."

"I like it fine." Once again those pale blue eyes seemed to seek hers for a moment, then drop in embarrassment. Somewhat stiltedly, he went to his meal. After taking it to the table, he offered a quick silent prayer of thanks, then he proceeded to eat without so much as warming it up for a bit in the oven.

Katie joined him. "So, how was your work at the lumberyard?"

"It was good."

She tried again. "Did you do anything interesting? What, exactly, do you make there, anyway?"

Wearily, he wiped his mouth. "We make shells. You know, lumber frames for homes. We have a large contract for a builder out near Toledo. We build furniture, too, sometimes."

"That sounds interesting," she murmured, though it didn't, not really. "Do you like it?"

"I like it well enough. My boss, Brent, is a good man." Jonathan turned his plate a quarter turn so he could continue to shovel in his meal. In sync with his fork hitting the plate, he shrugged. "There isn't much to say. The work is hard, but plenty. And the pay is *gut*, too. That's a blessing."

For a moment, Katie found herself noticing everything about Jonathan, all over again. The way he held his fork. The scar along the base of his thumb. The way his cool blue eyes seemed to always find hers. "Indeed. Well, I spent the day getting organized."

"Did you have any problems?"

"No. Not at all." She swallowed hard as once again his hand stilled and he looked long at her.

"*Um,* please don't worry about the girls. I will care for them just fine."

"I assumed you would."

"Oh. Well, then . . ." Her voice drifted off. When she noticed him shifting, about to leave the room, about to stand up, she blurted, "How did you get that scar?"

He stilled. "Which one?"

Before she could stop herself, she reached out and touched his thumb. His skin felt so different than hers, rough. Cool. He started from her touch. "That one."

"Oh. I cut it years ago when I was mending some fencing." He ran his other thumb across his hand, just like she had done.

"It must have been some cut." Feeling terribly girlish, she amended her words. "I mean, it's almost an inch long."

He looked at his hand as if he was looking at that scar for the first time. "I guess it was. It healed, though, and I'm right as rain." For a moment, their eyes met, and his expression gentled—almost like he cared about her. Then, just as suddenly, he stood up. "I . . . I am going to wash up now."

Stunned, Katie watched him pick up his plate, set it near the counter, then walk away. Leaving her alone.

As she looked around the suddenly silent kitchen, Katie thought that perhaps her parents had been right. Perhaps her stay here would be a thankless one, indeed. The girls were not eager to get to know her. The house was empty and far too quiet. Winnie would be gone soon.

And Jonathan . . . Jonathan seemed wary around her. Watchful. Almost bashful?

Chapter 6

Brandon was sitting up in bed half watching television when Holly arrived at the hospital that afternoon. Pausing at the door, tears pricked her eyes. For once, Brandon looked almost like his usual self. It had been a rough week—there'd been a few times when neither the doctors nor the nurses thought he would last to the next day.

There were times when she wasn't sure she'd be able to make it, especially since all the news was now increasingly dire. Holly was finding it hard to stay positive.

But of course, that was what he needed. "Hey, you," she said when she finally walked through the doorway. "How does it feel to sit up in bed for a change?"

With effort, he turned her way. "Pretty good. So, are you ever going to actually come in? I've been watching you stand there for five minutes."

"Sorry. My mind was wandering, I guess," she murmured, walking toward him. After squeezing his shoulder, she pulled up her usual chair and sat down next to him. "So . . . are you feeling a little better?"

"Yeah. I think those new drugs are helping with the pain."

His words told her everything she needed to know. He wasn't healing. A miracle wasn't about to take place. His prognosis wasn't going to change. He just wasn't feeling as bad as he usually did. "Oh. Good."

Brandon motioned to the remote control on the bedside table. "Turn off the TV, would you? I want to ask you about something."

"Anything," she said as soon as the screen went black.

"Did . . . did you ever get ahold of Katie? Did you find her?"

"No." Regret consumed her as she watched his expression fall. Oh, she'd give just about anything to have different news for him. "I wrote Katie a note and asked her to meet me on Sunday but she didn't show up." She'd waited three hours. As each minute passed, Holly's anger had intensified. It was just so unfair. Here Brandon was hoping to see Katie one last time before he died—and Katie couldn't even trouble herself to give Holly a few minutes of her time.

"Oh." With a sigh, his eyes drifted shut.

If Katie was standing in front of her at that minute, Holly knew she would have reached out and shaken her, hard. "I'll try again, Brandon."

For a long moment, the only sounds in the room were the plethora of machines that monitored his vital signs. At last, he spoke. "Why do you think she didn't show?"

"I don't know." When he tried to grip the electronic control to lower the head of the bed, she stood up and pushed the button herself, helping to adjust the pillows under his head as he shifted. "Maybe she didn't get the note. I had to leave it at the general store, you know. I'll go over there this afternoon and check."

"You don't have time. You've got work. I know you've got your job, Holl . . ." His words were slurring. Either the pain medicine was really kicking in or his body couldn't wait to rest.

"Sure I do." Reaching out, she clasped his hand. "I'll find her, Brandon. I'm going to find her and bring her to you. I promise."

His eyes still closed, he almost smiled. Almost.

Holly sat back down and watched her brother sleep. It was time to face the painful truth. They were almost out of time. No matter what—no matter what it cost to her pride or her feelings—she had to get hold of Katie.

Life was very different at Jonathan's home, Katie realized as she walked down the hall to the girls' bedroom one morning just days after Winnie had left with a smile and a wave before boarding her bus.

She missed the hustle and bustle of the inn as much as she missed her parents. At home, it was rare to find a moment's peace, never mind an hour of it.

"Girls, it's time to wake up," she said after poking her head in the door.

The two bundles under matching blue and yellow quilts hardly moved. Katie couldn't help but smile at how cute they looked. Their small sleeping forms brought back memories of her own childhood. Although, back when she was small, it had been Rebekeh's job to wake her up. Only Rebekeh's promise of hot chocolate would rouse her from slumber.

Softly venturing in, she gently shook each of them awake. "Mary, Hannah? It's morning."

Hannah rubbed her eyes as she sleepily sat up. "Katie?"

"Yes, dear. Time to get up."

Obediently Hannah sat up. "You look pretty today."

"*Danke*." Brushing a silky strand of hair away from Hannah's sweet face, Katie smiled. "You look *schlafrig*. Sleepy."

Just like she had the morning before, Hannah giggled, pushed back the covers, then scrambled out of bed. "Not any more! Good morning!"

"Good morning to you." Turning to Mary, Katie shook her shoulder gently. "Now, Mary, you must get up, too. The sun is waiting for you."

"I will." But still, she didn't move.

"Now, please."

Sullenly, Mary groaned. "I'm getting up. Where's *Daed*? Is he still here?"

"No, he left for work early today."

Actually, he'd left almost three hours earlier. She'd had to scramble to get downstairs and help him make his breakfast and lunch before he hitched up his wagon.

"Tell me when you want to eat breakfast in the morning and I'll have it ready for you," she'd said, once again trying so hard to be near him.

But instead of looking grateful, Jonathan had looked disconcerted in her presence. "You don't need to go to so much trouble. As a matter of fact, there's no need for you to be even getting up with me."

She'd chuckled. "You obviously have forgotten that I'm used to living at an inn. I've made breakfast for dozens of folks. You will not be much trouble at all." She'd opened the refrigerator. "How about some eggs and toast?"

"That . . . that would be fine."

"And lunch? Would you care for some soup and sandwich?"

"Anything would be fine, Katie."

She'd busied herself at the stove so he wouldn't see her blush. But she couldn't seem to stop her reaction every time he said her name, so slowly, with a slight lilt. Like he was drawing out every sound.

Clearing her throat, she fussed around the girls' room for another moment or so. "I'll see you when you get to the kitchen. Don't tarry too long."

"I'll hurry, Katie!" little Hannah said.

As expected, Mary said nothing.

Once again, Katie cooked a large breakfast. But just like the day before, the hearty meal of eggs and bacon, toast and fresh jam was a battle to get through. "These eggs aren't like Winnie makes them. Yours are too runny."

Katie knew she made a fine fried egg—there were dozens of guests at the inn who could testify to that. But she tried to look remorseful. "*Hmm. I'll try to do better tomorrow.*"

"I don't like this bacon, neither."

"You'll be hungry then, won't you?"

After a moment, Mary obstinately began eating, leaving Katie ready to go back to bed. With neither Winnie nor Jonathan there to run interference, Mary's jibes felt especially hard to take. She hoped Mary would back down from her one-girl war against her soon, because Katie knew her patience was near its end. One day soon she was going to retaliate with something mean right back.

Katie did her best, but the good Lord knew she was most certainly not perfect.

After breakfast was the usual running around, packing lunches and double-checking for all the homework supplies. Katie waved them off as they walked hand in hand to the Amish school, which was less than a mile away.

After the house was empty, Katie took the time to sip another morning cup of tea, then, without much more dillydallying, began her chores with a sigh.

This was when her day seemed the hardest.

She was used to the companionship of her mother, and the constant comings and goings of guests at the inn. Most recently, she'd had Anna— dear, talkative Anna. To Katie's pleasure, Anna had become her best friend in the world despite her few frustrations. Not only did they laugh and enjoy each other's company, making the tasks go by more quickly, but Anna also helped shoulder a lot of Katie's chores and work. Now, though, it was just her by herself. Katie found it lonely.

On her third day, just as she'd put on a kettle for tea, her mother came to visit. As soon as she opened the door and saw her, holding a large basket full of supplies, she burst into tears. "Oh, *Mamm*. I'm so glad to see you."

"*Ach*. Are things that bad?" she asked, curving a reassuring arm around Katie.

"Yes. No. Oh, I don't know." She stepped aside so her mother could enter, then followed her to the kitchen, where only half the dishes were cleaned.

Her mother looked at her in surprise. "Katie?"

"Things are so different here. Even though I'm

by myself, I'm having a heap of trouble keeping up with everything." She pointed to the barn. "The animals. The chickens. That goat."

Her mother chuckled. "That goat always was a nuisance. No one could ever get it to mind, even before we sold it to the Lundys. It gives good milk, though."

Katie shook her head in wonder. Obviously some things never changed. Leave it to her mother to mention that fact. "It's not just that. I can't seem to get everything done."

"You never had any problems at home."

"At home I always had you and Rebekeh."

Her mother almost smiled. "Careful, Katie, or you are going to sound as if you almost miss Rebekeh's bossy ways."

"I almost do." She held up a hand when her mother threatened to give into laughter. "Almost. Anyway, I guess I'm having trouble getting used to doing everything myself. Even working with Anna was a blessing."

"Many hands make quick work. But even the most industrious can not be expected to do the work of many, Katie. Perhaps you are being too hard on yourself."

"It's not the work. Well, not everything. *Mamm*, the hours drag by."

Understanding dawned. "You are lonely."

"I am. I'm sorry. I know that's not something I should complain about."

"I would find this solitude difficult, too, Katie."

"Really? You would?"

"Indeed I would." With a thoughtful smile, her mother murmured, "My goodness, the Lord knew what He was doing when he guided your father and me to open our house as an inn. I have a lot of joy in our constant stream of guests."

Katie's shoulders slumped. "I think I had joy there, too."

"Well, no matter. Soon enough you will be back."

"I suppose."

"You suppose? What does that mean?"

"I don't know. Maybe I'm destined to be a single woman, helping out at the inn. But what if that's not my future? What if things improve between Jonathan and me? What if one day he is interested in having another wife . . . and I find that I've fallen in love with him? What would I do then?"

"*Ah.* Those are tough questions." To Katie's surprise, her mother calmly considered the questions instead of just offering quick advice. "Katie, have you been praying?"

"I don't have time."

"That, my daughter, is the problem, don'tcha think?"

Katie didn't think so at all. At the moment, taking time out to say a prayer merely felt like one more thing to do. But she couldn't admit that. "*Mamm*—"

Her *mamm* hushed her, then took her hand and walked her to the only clean room in the house. The *sitzschtupp*, the living room, the good room that so far no one ever used. After sitting down beside her, her mother gently said, "Let us give thanks to the Lord our God."

They fell into silence, each praying with the Lord in her own way. A sense of peace filled Katie as she took time to give thanks for family and good health, for good neighbors and sunny fall days. As she relaxed and reminded herself that her life was in the Lord's hands, not her own, she felt all the stress from the past few days fall from her shoulders.

Her mother saw the difference instantly. "See now, dear? Nothing is so hard that it can not be shouldered with God's help."

"I do see. Will you stay for a while?"

"For a little bit. I brought you some things for the girls."

Katie was interested. "Such as?"

"I brought you your sewing and some new fabric. I thought you could help them work on a quilt."

Katie struggled to conceal her dismay. "*Mamm*, I just don't know—they haven't shown much interest in sewing."

"They will if you encourage it. Those girls will look to you for guidance, Katie."

"But what if they don't?"

"You won't know unless you try. And it will do

all three of you some good, to keep those little girls busy. They'll see your love for quilting and want to give it a try. I promise."

"But if they don't—"

"Then they won't. But in the meantime it might help all of you out." She looked at Katie carefully. "Don't you agree that busy hands help an eager mind?"

But what of sour dispositions? Yet, her mother did know so much. It was worth a try. "*Danke*, though I don't quite know how to get them started."

Her mother chuckled. "It is easy, dear. Simply pull out the fabric and tell them it is time to begin." Tenderly, she cupped her cheek. Her mother's hand was rough and strong, reminding Katie of just how much she'd done all her life to make their family life good and comfortable.

Had she ever truly appreciated her mother's sacrifices?

Leaving the basket in the living room, Katie followed her mother into the kitchen, where she efficiently put on an apron, then pushed up her sleeves and got to work on the dishes.

"Don't do those, *Mamm*. You have more dishes than you can count at home."

"Anna did them today. Together we will clean, Daughter, then we'll cook, *jah*?"

For the first time in years, Katie was grateful to get to work and be told what to do.

Chapter 7

That evening after the girls had their supper and they were waiting for Jonathan to return, Katie led the way into the living room. "Look what my mother brought over today—fabric." After sitting down on the couch, she spread a few of the especially beautiful pieces of cloth on her lap. The rich colors of butter yellow, dark red, and bright, vivid blue made Katie feel like she'd just brought the best of God's bounty into the room. "Aren't these fabrics pretty? Which one is your favorite?"

Hannah shyly pointed to the yellow.

Katie moved to place it on top of the others. "*Jah*, that is a wondrous color. It shines as pretty as the daffodils in May." Turning to Mary, she said, "Which one do you like?"

"None of them." Instead of sitting, Mary remained where she was, militantly glaring at the fabric like the swatches were terrible intruders infringing on her routine. "We're not supposed to be here in this room."

"Why ever not? It is a pretty room, to be sure."

"It is the *sitzschtupp*, our special living room. It is only for visitors."

It was on the tip of Katie's tongue to remind Mary that that was exactly what she was. She sure hadn't been treated like part of the family.

However, her mother's good example was fresh

in her mind, and that gave Katie the courage to push a little harder to make inroads. Sooner or later, Mary was going to have to bend a little, surely! "There's a mighty nice fireplace, we could ask your *daed* if we could make a cozy fire and begin work on a quilt tonight."

Though Hannah carefully nodded, Mary scowled. "He's going to say no."

"He might surprise you. All men enjoy a new quilt."

"I don't want to make a quilt. You're not going to make me do this, are you?"

"No, of course not," Katie said, but had a difficult time hiding her surprise and disappointment. Quilting had always brought her a great amount of joy. It was also something she felt proud about and comfortable teaching others to do. She'd been hoping to use quilting to forge a bond with Mary.

Meekly, little Hannah tugged on Katie's sleeve. "I do. Am I too small?"

"Not at all!" Opening her arm, she moved to one side as Hannah scooted closer. "I was younger than you when I pieced my first quilt. Mary, by the time I was your age, almost seven—why I was anxious to begin all kinds of projects."

Mary backed away, literally pulling away from her in both spirit and space.

However, Katie couldn't let Mary do that. If she didn't make the girl do anything she didn't want, they'd never make progress. And Katie really wanted to become friends with the little girl. "Come here, Mary, and give me your time, please. This task is important to me."

"No, I—"

"Please Mary. Sit down. I think you should try, yes? If not for my sake, then try working on this for my mother's. She was so hoping you would enjoy quilting."

Little by little, Mary unbent enough to come forward and join her sister.

With a glad heart, Katie watched Mary try her best to join in the activity. For an instant, Mary's behavior reminded Katie of her own. She remembered more than one occasion when her attitude had not always been pleasing or kind. Mary might be going through some of the same growing pains. In a worthy imitation of her mother, Katie stated, "We're going to start on this quilt. I've decided."

Mary's eyes narrowed. "*Daed*'s still going to be upset we're using this room."

"I will ask your father about it when he gets home."

At that moment, the back door opened wide. "Here he is," Hannah announced. "*Daed*'s home!"

Katie heard Jonathan carefully remove his coat and hang it up. "*Daed*, we're in the *sitzschtupp*," Mary called out.

Slowly, he walked to them. "Hi, Jonathan," Katie said, greeted him with a sunny smile.

Once again, he met her gaze, then cleared his

throat. Somewhat gruffly, he said, "What are you all doing?"

"I was showing the girls some fabric. I'm going to teach them to quilt." Katie grinned again, hoping her enthusiasm would catch on.

To her dismay, Jonathan didn't look encouraged. "They already have school, homework, and chores. Isn't that enough?"

Before Katie could explain how quilting gave her joy, not the burden of work, Mary snidely interrupted. "She wants to take over this room."

A muscle in his cheek jumped. "There is no reason for that."

Katie made a decision. "Girls, please go put your things away."

However, Mary and Hannah did not instantly obey. Instead they looked to their father for guidance. It was only after he nodded that they stood up and walked out of the room.

When they were alone, Katie motioned for Jonathan to sit. Like the girls, he seemed terribly reluctant to do so. Instead of leaning back in the chair, he perched on it, looking eager to rise and leave at a moment's notice.

"What is it about this room that makes you uncomfortable?"

"It doesna make me uncomfortable. It's rather that it is a special place. You see, it was Sarah's pride and joy." His words sounded bitter. Resigned.

To her eye, the room looked as plain and unwelcoming as the rest of the house. "It is a pleasing room, to be sure."

"I would rather you not dirty it."

"Since I am the one cleaning, I think that option should be up to me."

"The girls—"

"Need something to do at night," she interrupted crisply. "You read *The Budget*."

"Even Winnie—"

Katie was tired of being compared to his sister. "I'm sure Winnie had other things to do. Jonathan, when you asked for my help, you didn't say I had to follow your directions like a child." She stood up and stepped toward him, consciously pulling her shoulders back and lifting her chin. "I am not a child."

Something flashed in his eyes that she couldn't quite recognize. Embarrassment? Awareness? "I know you aren't, Katie."

Something about the way he said her name—the way he looked at her so directly—made her heart beat a little faster. She felt flustered and at a loss of words. Suddenly she wasn't all that sure what had upset her so much. "I . . . I had hoped we would be getting to know each other better, Jonathan."

As the air surrounding them thickened, he murmured, "We are."

A second passed. Two. Katie could hardly look away.

He spoke again. "I'm . . . sorry if I haven't seemed appreciative of your efforts. I . . . I am, Katie."

She wasn't sure what to say to that. So many feelings were brewing inside her, she felt disjointed, confused. Finally, she settled on claiming practicality. "Then, would you please help me build a fire in here? It would make this room cozy and welcoming. I'd like to instruct the girls on quilting this evening."

After a long moment where he seemed to be at war with himself, he finally nodded. Rubbing the scar on his thumb, he said quietly, "Katie, I did not plan for this."

She hadn't planned on many of the things that had happened at the Lundys'. She hadn't planned on feeling so alone, or having to constantly prove herself to the girls. She hadn't planned on being so aware of Jonathan's moods. Of being so excited to see him at the end of each day. Of the keen sense of disappointment when a meal passed and he'd hardly dared to look her way.

But things seemed to be changing. "I know you didn't," she murmured, wondering if he, too, might be feeling the pull between them.

"When I asked you here, I was only thinking of my daughters. I had only wanted you to watch over them."

"There's more involved with girls than simply making sure they are fed and clothed. I want to get to know them, and have them know me. Jonathan, I can't help being myself. I can't merely sit meekly for two months. That is not who I am."

"No, it's not." His eyes lit up. "I . . . I am starting to see that I hadn't known you before."

"I'm tired of being kept at an arm's length as if I'm hired help. It isn't fair. I came here as a friend."

Pain entered his eyes, like he'd known he'd been hurting her feelings but hadn't known what else to do. "I realize that."

"I've been terribly lonely. Won't you consider letting me in your life . . . if only as much as a little bit?"

Obviously at a loss for words, Jonathan swallowed hard, blushed mightily, then abruptly stood up, turned on his heel and left.

Feeling bemused, Katie watched him leave. Had she made any headway . . . or merely made things worse?

"Katie?"

Thank the Lord for Hannah! The little girl was peeking around the corner, her eyes wide and her mouth shaped in a little "o." "Come in, Hannah," she said with a smile. "We have much to do." Pointing to the fabric, she said, "We need to think about what size squares to make for our quilt."

Thumb hovering near her mouth, the five-year-old tiptoed in. "I havena seen my *daed* talk like that before."

"I did not mean to upset him."

Blue eyes blinked. "You just wanted your way?"

In spite of her jangling nerves, Katie laughed. "I suppose so. I guess I'm not quite as easygoing as everyone thought I was, *hmm?*"

Hannah sidled closer, her dark indigo dress brightening up the vacant room as much as her cheery personality. "You're different than Aunt Winnie."

"I know. She'll be back soon."

Hannah nodded, then picked up her favorite piece of fabric. In her arms, the buttery yellow stood in vivid contrast against the dark blue. "Winnie doesn't know how to sew."

"She can sew well enough, I imagine."

"No, she can't. She sends out for the sewing. She bought my *daed* a suit from Mrs. Yoder for his birthday."

Katie struggled to hide her surprise. No Amish woman was expected to be an expert at everything. Sure enough, there were many who bartered or traded goods to get unpleasant projects done. But sewing was as much a part of her family as baking shoofly pie for guests. It was hard to imagine Winnie not sewing at all. In fact, Katie distinctly remembered working on a quilt with Winnie when they were just girls.

But perhaps Winnie had never really enjoyed such activities? "Mrs. Yoder does fine work."

"Does Mrs. Brenneman do that, too?"

"No. My mother is a very fine seamstress."

After a moment's reflection, Hannah confided, "Mary said my *mamm* didn't like to sew, neither."

"I can teach you if you'd like to learn."

"We'll use this yellow?"

"Definitely. I think we'll make a quilt called Sunshine and Shadow. It's made up of light and dark squares. It's a very lovely pattern."

"What if you leave before it's done?"

Unexpectedly, the thought of leaving caused Katie's heart to tighten. Hannah's smiles and sweet nature had claimed her heart. Katie looked forward to more days of holding Hannah's hand when they went to inspect the goat after school. Of baking buttermilk cookies with her, of showing Hannah how to measure ingredients just right. "I'm close by," she murmured, realizing her voice sounded husky. "Even if I'm living at the inn, we'll still have sewing lessons then."

Finally satisfied, Hannah crossed the two feet that had separated them and scrambled up on the seat next to Katie. "I'm ready."

"Then I'm ready, too."

Together they looked at a pattern book her mother brought, so intent that Katie hardly noticed Jonathan had come back in and was building up a fire.

And she was not aware of the pure relief that crossed his features as he saw how Hannah had taken to her. Katie only concentrated on the girl next to her.

• • •

As Anna stood next to Henry at the counter of Mr. McClusky's store a week before Thanksgiving, she could hardly believe the differences in her life. Mere months ago, she had accompanied Henry there for the first time. But unlike now, she'd tried to stay in the shadows. Lurking. Afraid of being found. She'd also been fiercely doing her best to deny her feelings for Henry Brenneman.

No, that wasn't quite right, she decided. For the first two weeks or so, there wasn't much to deny. She'd made up her mind to not like him. And the feeling had been mutual.

But now, dressed Plain and very close to taking her vows to the church . . . and later to Henry, Anna felt at peace. Henry was a good man, good in his heart and strong and stalwart. Sometimes she didn't know what she had done to deserve this new life of hers.

The door opened, bringing in a trio of women, dressed in harvest-colored sweaters and wool slacks. One of the ladies had a turkey pin on her jacket. Another wore a diamond cross around her neck. Each was holding Amish-made crafts and candles.

They were tourists, obviously. And they were staring at Anna and Henry as if they were the major specimens of their science project. Their interest made Anna want to check for crumbs on her cheeks, but Henry merely nodded in their direction.

Mr. McClusky acknowledged the tourists with a gracious smile. "Ladies. Good afternoon."

"Afternoon," they chorused, all eyes still pinned on Anna and Henry.

"May I help you with anything?" Mr. McClusky tried to engage the ladies.

The tallest woman, the one with the turkey pin, shook her head. "No, thanks. We're just here to sightsee." She turned back to stare at Anna like she'd just discovered a great wonder of the world.

Anna felt the blood drain away from her cheeks. "Come," Henry said in German, pulling her away from the curious stares.

Anna wasn't aware she was holding her breath until they disappeared down the aisle.

Once in relative privacy, he stopped her. "Are you all right?"

"*Jah. Danke*," she murmured, only realizing after the fact that he'd spoken to her in Pennsylvania Dutch and she'd replied in the same fashion. "I *um,* didn't realize I'd be so uncomfortable being stared at."

"It is different outside of the inn, isn't it?"

"Yes. At the inn, it's your parents' home, so it feels like we're the hosts. Here, I feel so exposed and at their mercy."

"They mean no harm."

"I suppose. It's just that it's different at the inn."

He gently clucked his tongue. "Anna, the inn is your home now, too, yes?"

His sweet words made everything feel right again. No matter what, she was happy with Henry, and happy with how things were going with their life. She needed to remember that. "Yes."

"Let's pay for our things and go home." His voice seemed to linger on the word.

Contentment settled over Anna as she followed him to the counter and stood by while he paid for the pasta and flour that their kitchen had run out of. Taking his bags from Mr. McClusky, Henry said, "Good-bye, then."

"Bye, Henry, Anna," the older man said with a knowing smile, making Anna wonder if he, too, was thinking of not so long ago when she didn't quite fit into this world. Much like the "sight-seeing" ladies in the store. "Oh, I almost forgot." Sam McClusky's forehead creased. "Katie got another letter."

"Another?" Anna's hand shot out before Henry could claim it. She looked to Henry in alarm. *What was going on?*

Sam nodded. "Yeah. The first one came about ten days ago, right, Henry?"

"More or less."

As Anna looked at Henry curiously, Sam continued. "I have to tell you both, the girl who's been dropping these letters off looks pretty desperate. It ain't my business, but if I were you, Henry, I might talk to Katie. I wouldn't want to have some stranger looking for my sister the way she is."

Henry looked genuinely alarmed. "Thank you for the note, and for your concern." He frowned at the envelope in Anna's hand before facing the proprietor again. "When did you say the girl dropped this off?"

"Three or four days ago. She was asking all kinds of questions about Katie, about where she lives, what she does, but I put her off." With a self-satisfied smile, he waggled his white bushy eyebrows. "You know me, I'm not about to divulge anything to outsiders."

Anna knew she would be forever grateful for that character trait. "I know that for a fact, Mr. McClusky. You certainly kept your silence when Rob was after me."

"He was no good, Anna." Shaking his head in dismay, he added, "I still can't believe he tried to bribe me in order to find you."

"If he had known what kind of person you are, Rob Peterson would have never tried such a thing," Anna said. "I can't imagine you ever accepting a bribe. You are a *gut* friend, indeed."

"I appreciate your help," Henry said before ushering Anna out into the brisk wind. As they walked across the busy parking lot toward their buggy, he murmured, "Something isn't right."

Anna had a sudden desire to toss the envelope in the trash and never tell Katie of its existence. Turning to Henry, she asked, "Did she let you read the first note?"

"Nope. She got right angry when I tried to learn about the contents, too. Anna, Katie had quite a rebellious time during her running-around years. I'm wondering if her past has come back to haunt her."

Anna knew all about running from her mistakes, but yet, Katie was the sweetest girl she knew. "I doubt that. What did Katie do during her *rumspringa*, stay out late one or two nights?"

To her surprise, he shook his head. "Oh no. It was more than that. She'd go out almost every night. She wore makeup, too."

Anna couldn't help but chuckle. "Oh, Henry. That doesn't sound too strange. If you could have seen some of the girls in my ninth grade class— why the makeup they were trying out was crazy!"

"No, it wasna like that." He narrowed his eyes as he remembered. "It wasn't the makeup she wore, it was more the way she seemed to embrace everything about the English. And . . . her running around lasted a long time. My sister, Rebekeh, and I were sorely worried that we were going to lose her."

"Lose her? To what?"

"To the outside world." He held up his hand when it was obvious she was about to find offense. "Her leaving was a real matter of concern. She wouldn't talk to us about her new friends, wouldn't let even Rebekeh counsel her. She kept saying that we wouldn't understand."

"If it's her past that is bothering her, I know she won't get very far. I'm proof the past always comes back. You can't hide from it for long."

"That's what makes me *naerflich*. I think my sister is truly worried about being reminded of her past, but she won't let me help."

"I can understand you being nervous. Well, I'll go to the Lundy farm tomorrow and deliver the letter. While I'm there, I'll try to get Katie to tell me what all this means."

He glanced at her in gratitude. "You'd do that?"

She reached out to him, clasping his hand. "Of course I would. I care about Katie. She's like a sister to me."

But as she said those words, a deep sense of foreboding nagged at her. From the day they'd first met, Katie had felt like a sister. Last year, she'd spent hours confiding to Katie about Rob, about his abuse. All along, Katie had just been supportive and caring.

Why hadn't Katie ever given her even a hint that she knew what the outside world was like? That at times, she, too, had made mistakes and felt regret for her actions?

More important, why wasn't she trusting Anna now?

Chapter 8

"You are truly my best friend, Anna," Katie said as she led the way into the *sitzschtupp*, which she'd stubbornly taken over. She'd become tired of Jonathan's rules and hearing about how Winnie and Sarah had always done things. Though she might only be in the Lundy house for a short time, she was determined to at least try and fit in—walking around like an unwelcome guest had become mighty trying.

Because of that, she had made the front parlor a cozy area. After a few begrudging remarks, even Mary now seemed to look forward to their nightly lessons in measuring, cutting, and piecing together fabric. The result was cheery mix of three-inch squares waiting to be added to their Sunshine and Shadow quilt.

Anna patted the bright yellow, blue, red, and cream colored fabrics lovingly. "These are beautiful. I like the size of the squares, too. The last Sunshine and Shadow quilt I made, the squares were cut so small, it made my eyes dizzy just to look at it."

"The larger pieces are easier for the girls to manage. We're going to add wide borders, too."

"I think it's going to be pretty." With a winsome look, Anna sighed. "I've been hoping to do some quilting myself, but I haven't had much time."

"You've been busy with other things, things far more important than piecing together a new quilt, I'm thinkin'."

"I wish I had more to show for all the time I've spent studying." Anna grimaced. "Katie, I'm afraid my Pennsylvania Dutch isn't getting much better. What am I gonna do if I never learn that language? I promised Henry I'd do my best."

"And, you are doing your best, *jah*? Don't be hard on yourself, dear Anna. You forget that most of us learned Pennsylvania Dutch before English. And never at such an old age." As she heard herself, Katie felt her cheeks heat. "Oh! I mean old . . . I just meant that most Amish learn to speak Pennsylvania Dutch first."

To Katie's relief, Anna didn't take offense to the "old" remark. Instead, she looked relieved. "You're right. I forget how much of what I'm learning you practically take for granted."

"You shouldn't. I know neither Henry nor our parents ever forget your sacrifices. You've changed so much for Henry."

"I have changed, but not just for Henry. I've changed the way I look at things, and I have to admit that I do like this 'new' me. Well, most of the time. Other times, I feel so awkward, I'm sure that I'll never be comfortable."

"Don't fret so. At the end of the day, Henry wants you to be in his life, not a master of two languages."

"I don't seem to be mastering much. I ruined one of your mother's tablecloths yesterday. I scorched it."

"There's ways to fix scorches. I'm sure my mother told you."

"Not that mess. I ruined it something awful, Katie."

Katie did her best to keep a straight face. "It's just fabric. We all make mistakes."

Anna rolled her eyes. "Those horrible hens hate me. They peck my fingers something awful."

"That's because they know you fear them."

"Of course I do! Their jabs hurt! I don't know what to do about that. I think your *daed* has just about had enough of me and my accidents."

"I know that's not true." Reaching out, Katie clasped Anna's hand. "Hush, now. One day I'll tell you about all the things I've done wrong at the inn. And there's a great many things I've done wrong."

"Promise?"

Katie hid a smile. Anna's look of hope was almost comical. "I promise. Well, I will if you vow never to mention bread baking around Henry. He loves to recount my first attempts making clover-leaf rolls."

"I'll give you my word. Though I have to tell you that I'm very curious about what happened."

"I can only tell you that it involved too much yeast, too much salt, and a dining room full of paying guests." Katie shuddered at the memory.

"We went through a record amount of water that evening."

"Oh, Katie. You do make me laugh! I knew I was right to pay you a visit."

"Your timing couldn't have been better."

Immediately concern filled Anna's green eyes. "Why? Are you having a difficult time?"

Though Katie would have loved to cry on her friend's shoulder and tell all, she knew better than to give into such foolishness. She'd wanted to be at Jonathan's home. She'd fought and cajoled her way to be here. She certainly didn't want to seem ungrateful or flighty—or inept. Especially not after she'd been giving Anna so much advice about managing an Amish household.

However, there was one matter that she was justifiably nervous about. Something that made even the most exacting housekeeper shudder and fret about. "I just heard today that we will be hosting church services here in two weeks' time."

Anna's eyes widened. "Are you sure? I was sure Irene told me it was the Barrs' turn to host."

"The Barrs' youngest has been sick with tonsillitis. Now the doctor says the tonsils need to come out. In light of that, Jonathan volunteered his home."

"Oh, Katie. We have a lot to do."

That was somewhat of an understatement. Holding church services was a big undertaking. The whole house would need to be cleaned top to bottom, food prepared, and room made for the benches and tables. "Thank you for saying 'we.' "

Anna laughed. "Of course I'll help you. Why, we all will!" Looking around, she asked, "I haven't been here for church before. Where does Jonathan usually hold the services?"

Katie pointed to the door that led to the bottom floor. "In the basement. There's lots of room."

"Enough to seat two hundred people on benches?"

"Jonathan says so. Luckily, the area shouldn't need too much work to be ready to host. It's fairly clean and tidy and is sparsely furnished. There is also a door that leads outside so everyone won't track mud and dirt through the house. It's everything else that makes my stomach turn in knots."

"What do you plan to serve?"

"The usual fare. Coffee and tea to drink. Trail bologna sandwiches, with fresh bread and relishes. And of course, peanut butter and jelly for the *kinner*." Katie thought some more. "Oh, and cookies. I thought we'd have cowboy bars, oatmeal cookies, and snowballs."

"Your *mamm* and I can do the baking. We'll bake the bread and cookies."

"*Danke*. Some other ladies will come over next week to help me clean."

Anna reached out and clasped her hand. "Everything will work out just fine. I feel certain."

Katie smiled. "That's what I told Jonathan.

117

However, I have to warn you he didn't look as confident as you sound."

"He doesn't know you like I do. Remember, you are the woman who taught me to cook for a crowd. If you can do that, you can handle this."

"I'm glad you have so much faith in me." Turning back to the beautiful quilt fabric in front of her, Katie said, "But for now I want to spend some time on this quilt. That is important, too."

They both started organizing the fabric. It was almost impossible to sit still when there was quilting to do. Anna eyed Katie a little more closely. "So are you going to tell me how things are going?"

"You heard what I said."

"And, I also heard what you did not say. Come on Katie, this is me."

Anna was right. Maybe her ear really was what Katie needed. A friendly person to listen objectively. "All right," she said haltingly. "Things have been . . . more difficult than I had imagined."

"How so?"

"I don't rightly know. Things have been awkward in so many ways. I'm having trouble finding my place here. I had hoped that Jonathan and I might have some time together, but that seems like it will never happen."

"It's only been a few weeks."

But what an isolated time it had been! "That is true."

"How are the girls?"

"Confused. Hannah is a dear, but Mary harbors a lot of anger, I tell you. She doesn't trust me."

"It must be hard, losing her mother."

"I'm sure it is. There's been lots of other changes, too. Jonathan's working at the lumberyard has been a hard adjustment, I'm thinkin'. The girls were used to knowing he was close by even if they didn't see him."

After hesitating about whether to divulge more information, Katie decided to add some more. "And, then there's everything going on with Winnie."

Anna leaned forward. "I've been thinking a bit about her trip and that first meeting with Malcolm. Have you heard from her? Was Malcolm everything she'd thought he was going to be? Is she happy?"

"Anna! You sure you've only been thinking about her trip a 'bit'?"

"Okay. Maybe more than a little bit. Though we don't know each other too well, I do hope the best for her. I know how hard it is to jump into a new situation. So, what have you heard?"

Thinking back to the sound of Winnie's voice, Katie hedged. "Well, she called Jonathan at the lumberyard to let us know she arrived safe and sound. The Troyers have a phone booth at the end of their road to use for emergencies and such."

"I'm pleased to hear that, but I'm more curious

as to how she's finding Malcolm. Did she say? How are they getting along, face to face?"

Katie looked at her friend with a new awareness. "I'm now realizing that you are not terribly hopeful about Winnie's trip."

This time it was obvious that Anna was the one who was choosing her words carefully. "I'm hopeful that she finds happiness."

"But you don't think Winnie will?"

"I didn't say that."

"It's what you are not saying that interests me. Truly, Anna, you don't sound as if you hold out much hope for a happy ending for Malcolm and Winnie."

"I don't, not exactly. Before she left, Winnie seemed so eager to find Malcolm as everything she wanted. I'm afraid that she will either not see his faults or not take the time to really get to know him," Anna said, not looking away. "This sounds obvious, but people are hard to really know. Sometimes it takes weeks or months to see who the real person is. Sometimes first impressions can be so misleading."

"You are speaking of Rob, aren't you?"

Anna looked away. "It's hard for me not to think of Rob when I hear about Winnie's excitement to meet the man behind his letters. I mean, on the surface Rob looked polished and handsome and successful. He was running for a seat in the House of Representatives. It was only after we'd become serious that I realized how controlling and abusive he was. It's easy to only look at the surface of people. Far harder when you dig deeper. We all have so many layers on for reasons."

"Even Henry?"

Anna grinned. "Most especially Henry. He'd been hurt when Rachel left him for the *Englischer*. When we first started talking, I was sure he was just a sour, glum man."

"And he thought you were simply a spoiled, flighty fancy girl."

Anna looked serious again. "We were lucky, because we found out that our hearts matched and complimented each other. That isn't always the case, though."

"No, I imagine not."

Rubbing a worn spot on the wooden table, Anna added, "You might not know about this, but there's lots of stories in the news about men and women who pretend to be something they aren't on the Internet. That makes me wonder about this man's letters. Malcolm may have good intentions, but he may not be everything he says he is. It's only nat-ural to want to downplay a person's flaws."

"I don't believe Winnie is finding that to be true. While she hasn't sounded over the moon about Malcolm, she sounds happy enough in the letters we've received so far."

"I hope she will be."

"I do, too. Maybe we shouldn't worry so much,

Anna. I've learned that Winnie is a woman of strong will and character. She might want to be in love, but she is no *dummkopp*, no dunce. If this man has shortcomings, she'll discover them." Katie shrugged. "In any case, because of Winnie's trip, I think the girls are even more unsettled. I think they've overheard Winnie talk about her wish to one day be with Malcolm. To them, it's one more person stepping out of their lives."

"You'll win them over."

"With the Lord's help I might." Katie did not say that lightly. She was finding so many stumbling blocks, it would be a miracle if the girls and she reached common ground any time soon. Pushing the quilt project to one side, she stood up and smoothed her skirt. "I suppose I'd better get started on supper."

As they entered the kitchen, Katie motioned to a plate in the sink, where she'd set out pork chops to thaw. "I thought I'd season these for a bit before I bake them." Suddenly she doubted everything about herself. "Does . . . does that sound like a *gut* idea?"

Anna squeezed her hand. "You are a wonderful good cook. I imagine anything you make will be tasty."

Katie couldn't believe how much she needed to continually hear the praise. She'd always thought of herself as a strong woman, but at the moment, she'd never felt more alone and weak. "I thought

we'd have applesauce, too. I made some yesterday."

"All *kinner* like applesauce."

The Amish way of speaking of children perked
Katie right up. "You sound mighty *gut*, Anna. I bet
your guests at the inn think you are Amish, born
and raised."

Anna giggled. "As long as I can tell them about
where to shop, they are happy."

"And answer all their questions."

"Oh, all those questions! Someone asked me the
other day if I had an alarm clock in my room. She
had supposed a rooster woke me up every
morning."

Katie laughed merrily. "Oh, can't you see my
daed, having to fuss with a noisy rooster every
morning? We'd be having it for supper after a
week."

"I'd eat it, too. Well, as long as I didn't have to
cook it."

"Don't worry, Anna. No one would ask you to."

They laughed again, barely catching their breath
before Anna would mention another funny story
about one of the guests.

Impulsively, Katie reached out and hugged her
hard. "I'm so glad you came."

"Me, too." As the sense of true warmth and
friendship flowed through them, Anna's eyes
widened in alarm. "Oh my goodness, we got so
busy talking about things, I almost forgot to give

you this." She pulled a white envelope out of her patchwork tote bag.

From the moment she recognized the handwriting, Katie felt dizzy. "Where did you get this? Did it come to the house? To the inn?"

"No. It was left at McClusky's store. Sam handed it to Henry and me the other day."

Obviously Holly was still determined to talk to her. Why? It just didn't make sense. When she noticed Anna studying her carefully, Katie did her best to act nonchalant. "Well, thank you for delivering this. I'll *uh,* read it later."

"Huh?"

Katie felt her cheeks heat. Even to her own ears her words sounded stilted and awkward. "I'm sure it's nothing important. Thank you—"

Before Katie could reach for the envelope, Anna set it on the counter. "Enough with games. Henry said this was the second envelope you've received. What is going on?"

Struggling to keep her voice even and true, Katie said, "Nothing. I received a letter, Anna, not a bomb."

"I know something's going on. No one receives letters at a store."

"The Amish—"

"Don't 'Amish' me," Anna retorted crisply. "I may struggle with a lot of things, but like Winnie, I am no dunce. You have a mailbox. There's got to be a reason you're not receiving letters here at home. Tell me what is going on. Let me help you."

Shame, and the pure petrifying worry of what was in the letter, kept Katie from divulging all. Her past troubles were her own problems to bear—no one else's. "I am having some . . . difficulty, but it's nothing you can help me with."

"What kind of difficulty? And why wouldn't I be able to help you?"

"You wouldn't understand."

"Of course I would. Katie, I lived most of my life in the outside world and seen some shady sides of it." With a look of amusement, she added, "I've seen more hours of daytime television that you can imagine. Believe me, there's nothing you could say that would shock me."

Perhaps that was right. But Anna had one thing Katie never had—an openness about her. Katie always preferred to look as perfect as possible to the people in her community. By doing that, she was able to keep her private struggles to herself. And the plain truth was that there was nothing Anna could do to help her, anyway. She had made the mistakes. She was the one who had hurt people. Therefore, it was up to her to solve the problem. "I'm not ready to discuss it."

Anna stepped right through her fragile barrier and pushed some more. "Won't you at least tell me who is writing you?"

"It doesn't matter. You wouldn't know her."

Anna grabbed hold of the clue. "Why wouldn't

I? Sam said she looks desperate. Why do you think that is? What does she want? How did you meet her?"

The panic was back. Engulfing. "I meant . . . I meant . . . oh, stop, Anna! There's no reason for you to be involved."

"I care about you. I see how worried you are. That's reason enough for me to be involved." Reaching out for Katie, she gripped her arm. "So it's an English girl writing you?"

"Anna, I would rather not discuss it."

"Where did you meet her? At the general store? At Mr. McClusky's?"

"No."

"Where then? At the inn?"

"Let's not speak of it, please."

"But I'm confused. Katie, we used to write to each other all the time. I've also seen you chat with any number of *Englischers* at the inn. It seems strange that these letters you are receiving are bothering you so much. Who do you not want to speak to? Why does this woman not even know where you live?"

"I'd rather not say."

"Katie, I promise that you'll feel better if you let someone else share your burden."

"Anna—"

But still Anna fired off another question. "Are you worried someone wants to do you harm? Is it safe for you to be alone?"

As much as she hated to shoo away her visitor, Katie resolutely walked to the kitchen door and lifted Anna's coat off the peg. Having Anna involved would not solve Katie's problems and only bring a lot of new ones to Anna.

And no matter what she had done so far, at least she hadn't brought trouble into her friend's life. Anna didn't deserve that. No one did. Taking care to keep her expression blank, she said, "Thank you for stopping by and for delivering the letter. Thank you, also, for offering to help so much with the services."

"You're welcome. And, I'll share the news about you hosting with your mother, though I imagine she's most likely heard about it by now. Irene seems to know everyone and everything around here."

Katie knew that was almost true. "When Jonathan brings the wagon with the benches, dishes, tablecloths, and such, I'll look forward to your help."

"You can count on it." Reluctantly, Anna stood up. "Pushing your problems away doesn't solve anything, you know. They'll still be there until you face them. I know that more than anyone."

Anna shook her head. "I tell you, no one would ever guess how stubborn you really are, Katie. You look so sweet and innocent." With a small smile, she said, "Promise me you'll let me help you the moment you are ready to talk."

Katie liked how Anna phrased her offer. It

reminded Katie that Anna knew about keeping secrets and not always feeling able to share them. "I'll see you soon."

"Hold on. I could visit you tomorrow?"

"We both have work to do, Anna. I'll see you soon."

"But—"

Katie practically shut the door on her friend. "I'm sorry," she whispered to the thick wooden frame. "I'm sorry but I just couldn't take another question."

But more than that, she just couldn't make herself lie anymore.

Her body shuddered. She felt out of breath, like she'd just run a long distance in the cold. Yes, that was what her body felt like—frozen.

Outside the door, Katie heard Anna talk to Stanley, her buggy horse. She couldn't help but smile at her friend's chatter. Anna was truly determined to treat her buggy horse like a pet.

Still the letter waited.

Time had proven that pushing things off to the side didn't make things go away. No, it just delayed what was bound to happen. With thick fingers, she tore open the letter.

This time only a few hastily written words greeted her.

WHY DIDN'T YOU MEET ME? Katie, this is important. I won't go away. Meet me at the Brown Dog on Sunday. Please.

I won't go away.

That was a threat, indeed. It also sounded much like a fact. For whatever reason Holly had, she was not going to give up or give in. And unfortunately, she felt very sure that Holly did intend to find her. After all, what did Holly have to lose?

Katie had so much to lose. After she'd spent one agonizing night thinking about how her life would be if she never joined the order, Katie had made the decision to tell everything to Holly and Brandon and never see them again.

After Holly had gone between tears and anger, and Brandon had simply stared at her in shock, Katie had gone home and tried to be the person her mother had raised her to be. If all the truth came out—about how close she'd come to giving everything up for Brandon—Katie felt like she'd lose everything she was and everything she'd tried so hard to be.

And what about Jonathan? Would he not want a woman like that raising his girls? Perhaps every hope she'd had for a life with Jonathan would vanish into thin air.

It was impossible to think of. It was all she could think about.

Feeling dizzy and sick, Katie rushed to the door and scrambled outside. Ready to share the awful note with Anna after all.

Ready to accept help.

To seek advice. To tell someone—anyone—all

about everything she'd done and every horrible choice she'd made.

How she'd taken advantage of Holly's friendship. How she'd let Brandon imagine she returned his feelings. How she'd lied to her family because she enjoyed Brandon's admiration. But as she looked for Anna's buggy and prepared to call out to her to stop, her heart lodged in her throat.

Anna had already left. Once again, Katie knew she was all alone.

Chapter 9

All day Jonathan had looked forward to the moment he could come home from work and relax in the comfort of his own home. But as he entered the living room and eyed Katie's gently curving shoulders and pale neck bent over a bit of sewing, he felt his face heat up.

Oh, Katie affected him so.

In fact, every time he heard her voice or spied a bit of her pretty form, he could feel himself becoming tongue-tied and the muscles in his shoulders starting to bunch. No matter how hard he tried to not be different around Katie, things were out of his hands. The plain truth was that he fancied her. He couldn't help himself.

And that wasn't right. He had no need to marry again, well, beyond his girls needing a new mother. But that didn't seem like a sound reason in the long run. Jonathan didn't plan on being married to a woman he wasn't sure he could love.

And fact was, he wasn't sure if he was capable of loving again. Did the Lord desire a man to do such things? His will was a mystery to Jonathan.

Yes, his feelings about Katie most certainly did not make sense. Surely if he was meant to marry again, it would be to a woman not so different from his first wife.

Someone not so terribly young and fresh and merry.

Though, perhaps he didn't need a copy of Sarah, after all.

Things with Sarah had been rocky at times, that was the truth. Her sharp tongue had cut his feelings more than a time or two. Their union hadn't been all that he had hoped it to be. His efforts to hide their strained relationship had been a surprise, as well. Jonathan had always prided his honesty and forthrightness. He'd thought those two qualities were integral to the type of man he was. But during those last months with Sarah, he'd been a master of doublespeak and avoidance.

Even his *gut* friend Eli had commented on it one evening when they'd been raking gravel for the church services. "What is going on with you, Jonathan?" he'd ask time and again. "You seem so quiet and blue. How can I help?"

But instead of seeking Eli's advice and assistance, Jonathan had brushed him off. He'd been too embarrassed about the state of his marriage. Too ashamed that he wasn't happier.

Now, though, Jonathan realized that in spite of his intentions, his heart and head were thinking about companionship again with a certain blue-eyed woman. Every time she smiled, he imagined a life with her. Every time she laughed, he'd find himself dreaming about the possibility of not being alone night after night, with only his shadow for company.

But was Katie Brenneman the answer? Part of him thought she could be. Katie had a sunny nature which encouraged him to smile. He liked the way she treated others and how she was just bossy enough so as he wouldn't be tempted to run roughshod over her.

She also had a winsome way he found as beguiling as anything he'd ever come in contact with. It made him want to protect her and keep her safe.

Though he was not anxious to admit it, he liked how she did not always bend to his will. She stood up to him, but not in that brash way Sarah used to. No, it was more Katie's way to listen to him, then state her reasons for wanting things differently.

She was a surprisingly good negotiator, that Katie.

In spite of himself, he smiled. As every day passed, Jonathan found himself becoming more eager to see her. Every morning when she made him breakfast, it was becoming harder and harder not to admire the way she moved about the kitchen so competently.

Not to notice how pretty her skin was when the morning light shined on her just so. How her clothes smelled of lemons and her eyes were bluer than a fresh spring iris.

But in spite of his awareness of her, he still found himself to be at a loss for words around her. Part of him wanted to encourage her attentions, to show her that he welcomed them. But old hurts from his past would curb his tongue.

Now he worried that his distant manner had wiped out any feelings she'd previously had for him. Would she now even want such a man as himself? Someone so much older than she? Katie was twenty, while he was twenty-eight. Eight years was a fair difference. Perhaps she would notice his age over time.

He'd also noticed how she had tried to please him. She'd taken to making applesauce bread when he'd commented how much he liked it. But, had he even attempted to praise her cooking skills? He doubted he had—sometimes when he looked at her, all thoughts would run from his head and it would take all he had just to remain in the same room with her.

Fact was, from the time he could remember, people had commented on Katie's fair beauty, both in looks and in spirit. While it was true rumors had circulated about her running-around years and how she'd been a bit too wild, Jonathan had long since pushed those stories off. Gossip seemed to be inevitable in their small community. No, Katie Brenneman was a fair faultless woman, and therefore, most certainly not the type of woman for him.

The only remedy he could think of for his preoccupation was to keep away from her. He decided to do just that, and began edging backward out the doorway. Perhaps he could read through *The Budget* again. There might be some article or bit of news he'd overlooked the first time he'd read it through.

Or he could work some in the barn. He'd neglected the tack room something awful lately. Blacky's bridles could use a good oiling.

"Jonathan, please don't go."

Caught, he froze. "Hello, Katie. *Gut-n-owed.*"

"Good evening to you, too."

Something in her voice was different. High strung. Concerned, he stepped forward in spite of himself. "Are you needing something?"

"No, it's not that." She treated him to a ghost of a smile. "I just—well, I was alone all day and now the girls are asleep. Want to come in here and sit for a bit?"

He did not. What would he have to say to her that she would find interesting? What would she do if she caught him staring at her, like a young boy?

She nibbled on her lower lip. "I won't keep you too long. I promise."

He couldn't refuse such an offer. "All right."

Katie was a near wonder—he'd feel bad if he didn't try to nod to her wishes at least a little bit. He moved forward and hesitantly sat in the large rocking chair across from her. "Are you warm enough?"

The fire was roaring, and she'd even thoughtfully laid a crocheted afghan along the back of his chair. "I'm comfortable. This room has become mighty cozy, don'tcha think?"

The room had never looked so inviting. But if he admitted that, it would shame Sarah's memory. Wouldn't it? "The fire is warm."

Something faded in her expression. Raising her chin, she tried again. "That rocking chair there is a fine piece of furniture. Have you had it long?"

He paused to rub the soft, buttery wood under his arm. "*Jah*. My *daadi—my grandfather*—made this chair soon after he and my *mammi* Leonna married."

"What kind of wood is it? Oak?"

"Oak, *jah*. But it's stained a fair shade." Remembering Sarah's criticisms of it, he mumbled, "Some think it's a bit too dark."

"It's beautiful. I've taken to rocking in it when the girls come home and want to read with me."

The homey bit of information brought forth inviting visions of the way he'd always envisioned his life being. Of security and comfort at home. Of his house being more than it was now—a shell of a place. "Mary and Hannah enjoy sitting with you, Katie. You've done much to help them."

"I like being with them."

"They can tell. You are so . . . so chatty." Jonathan closed his eyes as he felt his cheeks burn yet again. *Chatty?* For goodness' sake!

But to his great surprise, Katie acted as if he'd just given her the greatest of compliments. She laughed. "I know I'm too chatty! Henry has told me more than once that I am too talkative by half. It's a failing of mine, to be sure."

"We don't think so." Jonathan felt the blood rush to his face once more. Would she notice that he'd included himself in the compliment?

Hesitantly, Katie ventured, "To be honest, I miss my family."

Like glass breaking, the tender moment was shattered. "I'm sorry—but it's only for a short time that you will be here." Somehow he knew the place was going to seem even emptier than it had felt before Katie, with her bright blue eyes and winsome demeanor claiming every corner.

She blinked. "No, that isn't what I meant at all. I was going to say that I miss the way my family gathers together in the evenings. We read or quilt or knit. It's a very pleasant time."

Jonathan didn't know if he could sit with her in the same room for hours on end. With nothing to occupy himself except for the distraction of her smile and the girls. "I've never been much for reading anything besides *The Budget*."

"We could do other things." Eagerly she looked around. "We have puzzles at the inn. I could bring over one of those. Once Henry and I completed a two-thousand-piece jigsaw. It took us weeks!"

Just the image of sitting next to her, putting pieces together side by side made his throat feel dry. "I don't have—"

"Or any kind of game?"

He could see he was not about to get out of her suggestion so easily. "I'll do some thinking about that."

To his surprise, Katie chuckled. Intrigued, he asked, "What is so funny?"

"You are! *Of course* you are going to have to think about things, Jonathan. You do everything slow. As slow as molasses."

That sounded mighty critical. Stung, he said, "There's nothing wrong with takin' my time."

"There's nothing wrong with walking backward, either," she said with another chuckle. "I'm just surprised that you never want to shake things up a bit."

"My life has been shook enough, Katie."

All merriment fled from her face. "Oh! Jonathan, wait! I'm sorry! I didn't mean to hurt your feelings. Surely you know I was only joking?"

Embarrassment made his tone sharp. "My feelings are not hurt." And how could he even imagine telling her if they were? She'd probably laugh even more!

"So, please stay for a bit. We have much to discuss . . . to plan for the service."

"We've already planned most everything, *jah*? Eli and Henry will help me prepare the outside so there will be plenty of room for all the buggies and horses. They're also going to help with a path to the basement door. You said you had the menu in hand."

"I do, but I'm still worried."

"Many hands will make quick work of it all." To his surprise, he found himself speaking gently with her, like he would to Mary.

Like Mary, she responded to his encouragement. Sitting up a little straighter, she nodded. "You're right, Jonathan. Many hands will help. Yesterday afternoon the girls and I swept the basement well and washed the walls. Things already look better."

"The wagon with the oak benches will come tomorrow. Several men are going to help me unload them and carry them inside. Then, together, we'll wipe down everything until it shines."

She frowned. "It's too bad it's winter. I always enjoy the services when they are in a barn and we get to eat outside."

Almost naturally, he sought to calm her fears. "This will be nice, as well, Katie. Don't worry so. Plus, everyone knows our circumstances and will not judge too harshly if everything is not as perfect as it could be. You can't help that Winnie is gone and the Barrs had to cancel."

Her blue eyes sparkled. "I'll try to remember that. *Um,* how is Ruth, by the way? Did she recover from surgery all right?"

"I stopped at McClusky's for some supplies and heard the latest. Ruth did fine and now she is hoping for a lot of ice cream."

"I do love ice cream. It almost makes me wish I had a reason to enjoy a steady supply of it."

She liked ice cream? That was an easy enough way to make her smile. And, well, she was doing so much for him—it was the least he could do in return, right? "I'll bring you home some tomorrow, if you'd like."

To his pleasure, Katie blushed. "Oh. Well, thank you."

"Any special flavor you like?"

"Strawberry?"

"I like strawberry, too." Just as he was about to close his eyes in frustration—he sounded terribly young and foolish—Katie smiled. He felt her regard to his toes. Perhaps Katie and he might one day have a future, after all.

Reaching into a large basket, she pulled out the latest edition of *The Budget.* "Would you like to read for a bit? We don't have to talk anymore if you'd rather not."

At that moment, Jonathan trusted his eyes to

focus on the paper instead of his tongue to say the right words. "I . . . yes. I'd like to sit here and read with you. If only for a bit."

"Only for a bit is fine with me."

As the glow from the kerosene lamps mixed with the glow from the fire, the room became illuminated in warmth. A sense of calmness filtered through the air, mixing with the apple-scented candle and igniting his senses.

Finally Jonathan was able to admit to himself that this was the scene he'd always pictured in his mind, the type of moment he'd always wished he and Sarah had had more of.

After years of wishing for companionship, years of resigning himself to a lifetime of being alone, Katie Brenneman was showing him that there was still time to find love again.

She was someone he could trust his heart to. And that knowledge was incredible, indeed.

Chapter 10

I won't go away.

Katie bolted upright in bed and scanned the room, searching in the dim light for Holly. She'd heard the words so clearly, for a moment she'd been sure Holly was in the room with her. Her pulse beat rapidly, every muscle felt on alert. Taking deep breaths, Katie willed herself to settle down.

She also realized she'd come to the inevitable truth. It was time to meet Holly. Avoiding her wasn't working—all avoidance did was foster feelings of guilt and sleepless nights.

Surely, anything was better than receiving her notes from Henry and Anna and being faced with their questions.

But of course, she was alone. Katie shivered. In spite of the cold weather, her body was covered in sweat. With a grimace, she pulled at the neckline of her nightgown. It felt too snug and confining. Damp.

Little by little, as the chilly air met her skin, the dampness dissipated. She looked at the clock near her bed, its plain white face illuminated by the moonlight. Barely could she make out the numbers. Two a.m., or near that. Too early to get up. Four a.m. would arrive soon enough.

With a force of will, Katie lay back down again. But though she closed her eyes and breathed deeply, sleep was far away.

All that seemed to enter her mind were the awful words. Holly's sentences were as completely puzzling as they were frightening. "I won't go away"?

Why would Holly write such a thing? They hadn't seen each other in almost a year. What could be so important now? The only thing Holly could be speaking of was Brandon, and Katie knew it would be terribly foolish to ever see him again.

Sleep was surely never to come. After lighting a candle, she pulled out her memory box. The little teddy bear with the golden eyes stared back at her when she lifted the lid.

Gingerly, she held it in her hands, stroking the soft fur. Remembering how she'd felt when Brandon had placed it in her hands. Even now, she was reluctant to part with it. Such sweet moments were rarities.

"It's for you," Brandon had whispered. "It's just a silly toy, but it reminded me of you."

She'd sat there, mesmerized. "How did such a thing make you think of me?"

His expression teasing, Brandon had tapped the bear's head. "First, it's very cute. Like you." He'd leaned closer. "There there's its eyes."

She'd been completely confused. So terribly naive. "Mine are blue, Brandon. This bear's eyes are brown."

He'd laughed. "But they're almost as pretty. And they have a look of wonder in them. Just like you do, Kate. I love your sweetness. I like you so much. "

She'd closed her eyes then. Every sense had been aware of him. He always smelled like cologne. His feelings had always been so open toward her. So caring, as if she was special.

"Oh." She'd looked around the room for something to comment on, for something to say so she wouldn't sound so tongue-tied, but nothing else held her attention. Holly had left them to talk on the phone to one of her friends. That meant the two of them had been alone, with only the television to act as a chaperone.

Very gently, he placed the bear into her hands, like she mattered the world to him. "No matter what happens, take it, Kate. I bought it for you. Whenever you look at it, you can think of me."

"I won't need the bear to recall you."

Her frank words had made him chuckle. Oh, she'd always taken his words so literally! "You might."

And so, she had held that bear in her arms. She'd kept it even after he'd told her he loved her. Even after she'd told them the truth about who she was.

Even after she told them that she didn't love him. Not enough, anyway.

To her shame, Katie had encouraged his attentions. She'd smiled and flirted and hinted that she wanted everything he did.

Yes, she had disregarded everything she'd known to be morally right. She'd lied to her new friend, and instead of feeling vaguely guilty about hurting Holly's brother, Katie had felt triumphant. Important. Oh, so very full of herself.

Looking back, Katie wondered how she could have gone so far astray.

"Thank you," she'd said, giving the bear a little hug.

"Thank me with a kiss, Kate."

Kate. Brandon had called her Kate only a few times. But each time had felt special. Like she was part of his group, and had a nickname like all the others.

Like she belonged with him. And because she wanted it, too, she'd leaned closer and kissed him. His arms had curved around her. His hands had rubbed her back, then skimmed her body, his touch heavy and sure. Within moments, that kiss had become heated and out of control.

Almost.

In the flickering candlelight of her temporary bedroom, Katie flinched. What had possessed her to encourage him so?

Because it had been exciting? Because it had felt wonderful to be wanted?

Because no matter how much she'd smiled Jonathan Lundy's way, he'd only looked blankly back at her in return, his grief too overpowering to notice anything else?

And, yes, she had started to think about Jonathan a fair bit. After Sarah had died when Katie was almost nineteen, she'd seen him at community functions after a few weeks of isolation. He'd looked so stalwart. So alone. She'd begun to dream about helping him. Imagine being the one to make him smile again.

And though she'd thought she'd been rather secretive, it had been fairly obvious to everyone around.

Especially to her sister, Rebekeh, who was always so practical and always so blunt. After spying Katie's infatuated gaze for a good long minute, she'd nipped those dreams of infatuation. "Jonathan is not yours, and never will be," she'd said after Katie had almost embarrassed herself by eyeing Jonathan from across the way one Sunday after church.

"I know that." But, in truth, she had hoped that one day he would look over and notice her, too. Especially since no one at the gatherings had ever stirred her interest before.

No one had except Brandon, and she'd always known he wouldn't be an acceptable beau.

"Do you? You don't look that way. You look like you're imagining a life with Jonathan." In her usual, no-nonsense way, Rebekeh made a proclamation. "Mark my words, that's not going to happen."

"It might. One day I bet he's going to want another wife. One day he's going to want someone to help raise his daughters."

"He has Winnie to help."

"Winnie isn't going to want to live with them forever."

In reply, Rebekeh had merely handed Katie a casserole dish to carry to the picnic table. "You don't know that. What you are thinking is mighty wrong, Katie Brenneman. You'd do best to put it out of your pretty head."

Katie had tucked her head in shame but couldn't seem to help her wayward thoughts.

When Sarah died, Katie had already been enjoying her *rumspringa* for a year. She'd been enjoying Brandon's attention, though she'd also begun to feel wary around him. It was becoming obvious that Brandon felt far more serious about her than she did about him.

Then, she'd started imagining a future with Jonathan, Mary, and Hannah. And those day-dreams had been hard to shake.

Especially the dreams about being his wife.

She'd imagine saving him, removing his worried frown, taking her place in the community as a mar-ried woman. She'd think about raising his daugh-ters, and to have more *kinner* of her own. She'd picture what it would be like to look across the dinner table and feel his approval. To receive warm, sweet glances from him, the way Brandon looked at her. To be loved. For him to want her as his wife.

Outside a wind blew through the trees, brushing two stray branches against the windowpane. Reminding her of the bitter truth. As one month passed into two, then three, Katie had begun to respond to Brandon.

He'd made her feel special and pretty. Though she'd never intended to have a serious relationship with him, never had seriously doubted joining the church one day, she'd enjoyed pretending that she was emotionally involved.

And then late that night when she'd received that bear, after Brandon had told her how he loved her, everything had fallen to pieces. She'd confessed who she was. She revealed how she never intended for their friendship to be anything but a fleeting experiment of sorts. And when Holly had looked at her, so hurt and upset, when Brandon stared at her in shock, why, Katie felt the truth fall over her, plain as day.

She'd intentionally set out to deceive them and had succeeded.

However, the fact that she'd finally acknowledged the truth didn't justify her actions or make them easier to accept.

Suddenly, all she'd wanted to do was run. Katie had grabbed that bear, run to the front door, thrown it open, and burst out into the night. As she made her way home, she'd vowed to start over again. She almost had.

In the dark chilliness of the terribly bare guest room, her head began to pound. That had been months ago. She'd moved on with her life. It was time the doubts and self-recriminations moved on, too.

But still she felt restless and unsettled. Thinking herbal tea might be the answer, Katie hastily wrapped herself in a thick robe and slippers and padded to the kitchen. She'd just filled the kettle with water and set it to heat on the stove when Mary came in.

"What are you doing?"

For once, Mary didn't sound accusing. Instead, her voice merely sounded sleepy and young and curious. "Heating water for tea. I couldn't sleep. What about you?"

The little girl moved closer, her thick rag-wool socks muffling her steps. "I couldn't sleep, neither."

Katie noticed Mary's eyes were suspiciously bright, as if she was on the verge of tears. If it had been Anna, she would have hugged her friend and demanded to know the problem.

But things weren't quite that easy with Mary. The girl was as prickly as a porcupine and sent barbs her way just as frequently. Gently she stated the obvious. "You've got school tomorrow. You need your rest."

Mary merely shrugged. "I know." To Katie's surprise, the girl pulled out a chair and sat down. "Can I have some tea, too?"

"Sure." When the water boiled, Katie strained some chamomile, then carefully carried two mugs to the table. "Here we are. Be careful now, it's hot."

Almost in unison, the two of them blew on the hot brew, then sipped. The feel of the hot water sliding down her throat felt good and immediately calmed her insides.

Mary looked to be enjoying the brew as well. Tentatively, Katie asked, "Are you excited about hosting church on Sunday?"

"*Jah*. We are all going to play hide-and-seek after we eat."

"Henry and Rebekeh and I used to do the same thing. I really looked forward to hosting church, though it is a very big job."

Mary took another sip, then a third. "We worked hard in the basement."

"We certainly did. You and Hannah were mighty *gut* helpers. The floor is bright and shiny clean."

Solemnly, Mary said, "We might have to sweep again after the benches are put in."

"I imagine so. Well, we'll have to hope that the weather stays cold. If it warms up, we're going to have mud to pick up!"

Mary's eyes widened. "Katie, we'd be cleaning all week."

"Yes, indeed we would. But I have a feeling you and Hannah would make even that messy job a joy."

"Maybe," Mary agreed, then sipped again on her tea. After she set her mug down, she looked at Katie with eyes that showed she'd experienced quite a bit during her seven years. "You know, things are different with you here."

"Are they?" Used to Mary's stinging criticism, Katie braced herself to hear what awful thing she had done now.

"Even getting ready for church feels different."

Since Mary didn't sound critical, Katie sought her advice. "Am I forgetting to do something with the house? What does Winnie usually do to get ready? Does she do more in the basement than we've done?"

"I don't think so." Mary shrugged. "No, I'm not thinking about church." Mary sipped again before expounding. "See, when Winnie is here, it was more like when my *mamm* was alive."

"I know you miss your *mamm*. She was a wonderful woman."

Mary's cheeks pinked as she looked away. "I miss her. But, it's not that."

"I see." Tentatively, Katie tried again. "Your mother and Winnie were *gut* friends, weren't they?"

Mary nodded. "They were."

"That is a fine thing. It is a blessing when family gets along well. I like my sister's husband, Olan, very much."

Still struggling with her attempt to say what was on her mind, Mary pursed her lips. "That's not what I meant." She waved a hand, obviously trying to search for words not on the tip of her tongue. "You . . . you've shaken everything up."

Katie felt shaken up at the moment. "I'm sorry you feel that way. I've been doing the best I can for you, but I can't be someone I am not. I can only be myself."

"*Daed* said that, too."

That was news. Katie hadn't realized Jonathan had spoken to the girls about her. "Does he think that is bad?"

Mary shook her head.

When the silence stretched, Katie said, "Well, soon things will be back to how they used to be. Soon I will be gone and Winnie will return." Katie tried to keep her voice upbeat, but it was hard.

"Katie, I . . ." Mary sipped again, almost hiding her brown eyes as she did so. Mumbling around the rim of the ivory mug, she said, "I like you here. That's what I'm tryin' to say."

"You do?" To her great surprise, Katie's eyes filled with tears. Lately, she'd been so worried about her past and her future, and so torn with insecurities about how she was managing everything day to day, she hadn't even hoped to hear good news from Mary. "I can't tell you how happy I am to hear that."

"You don't look happy, you look sad."

"I'm happy. I promise."

Reassured, Mary said, "You know so much and are so pretty, I like being around you. I like learning to quilt." She rushed on. "You cook a lot of good food, too. I know my *daed* likes it."

Katie felt a rush of pleasure. "How do you know?"

"Sometimes he comes home early to eat dinner with us. He used to never do that. Now, though, he acts like he's waiting on you." Mary raised a brow. "Did you make him do that? Make him join us for dinner?"

"No. But I am glad he comes in. My family eats together every evening."

151

"Even with all those people there?"

"Especially with all those people there. Like the Lord, our loved ones need some special time carved out."

Mary sipped her tea as she continued to stare at Katie thoughtfully. "Hannah seems happier, too. She used to cry a whole lot more."

Katie almost asked what was the source of Hannah's tears, but for the first time in a long while, she bit back her impulse and sought patience instead. "I'm glad Hannah is not crying so much."

"Me, too. There was no way I could make things better. My mother is gone to the angels."

"Yes, she is."

Eyes wide, Mary whispered, "Why do you think God took her from us so early? We all ride in buggies. Why did she get hurt and no one else?"

"I don't know."

Mary slumped. "I guess I'll have to ask when I get to heaven."

That made Katie smile. "I don't know if our eternity goes that way. I would think it would be mighty time-consuming for our Lord to sit and answer questions."

"I'm not going to take up too much time. I just want to know why."

"Put that way, I suppose it's a reasonable request."

Their tea was almost done. Staring at the scant

bits of tea that had seeped through the wire mesh and sunk to the bottom of her mug, Katie said, "We should probably be getting to bed now. It's near three in the morning. Are you more tired?"

As if on cue, Mary stifled a yawn. "No."

"Something tells me that might not quite be true."

In a rush, Mary blurted, "What if you wanted to stay longer? What if we wanted you to? If we were to ask you to? Would you do that?"

To her surprise, Katie didn't know the answer to that. Would she want to stay with Mary and Hannah out of duty? To stay only as someone who could look after the house? "The answer to that would depend on your aunt and father. Remember, we don't know what is going to happen with Winnie."

"She might move to Indiana."

"But she might not. She went out there to get to know Malcolm, and to get to know his family. Not to make plans."

"But what about you? If my father said you could stay here with us, what would you say?"

There was the question. A few months ago, Katie would have thought she'd do anything to attract Jonathan's regard. During her first few days at the Lundys', when she was so sad and lonely, she would have said she couldn't wait to return home. Now, though, she wasn't sure what the future had in store for her.

"I don't know," Katie finally murmured. "But I will tell you this: it is better to not always think about the what-ifs in life. If you give yourself to the Lord, then He will make clear all the hard decisions, and we won't have to worry about so much. Remember, the future is in God's hands, not ours."

Mary scowled as they set their mugs in the sink and started up the stairs. "When do you get to be old enough to have your future in your own hands?"

Instead of reminding her again of the Lord's will, Katie chuckled. "You, Mary, remind me of myself. So impatient."

"Really?"

"Really." Cupping Mary's shoulder as she paused, Katie added, "I have always been in a hurry. I used to shame my mother with my impulsiveness. I got into trouble a time or two at school as well."

"I didn't know that."

"That's because we don't know each other well. Maybe soon we will."

There'd been a time when Katie had felt that she was in control of everything. Now she was smarter and stronger. Now she realized that she wasn't in control of anything. Her future felt as slippery as ever. "But, to answer your question, I don't know if we ever get old enough. Our future is in the Lord's hands. It's best to remember that, don'tcha think?"

"Maybe."

Katie reached the landing and turned to Mary. "It's time we slept. Morning will come even if we're not quite ready to greet it."

Mary nodded solemnly, then to Katie's surprise, reached out and wrapped her arms around her.

Automatically, Katie hugged her back. The little girl's arms felt wonderful wrapped around her waist. Bending down, she pressed a kiss on her head. Yes, the Lord did work in mysterious ways.

"Ready for the weekend, Jonathan?" Brent called out at five o'clock on Friday, just as Jonathan was slipping on his coat and gloves. "I feel like it's been the longest week imaginable."

"It has been tiring, for sure," Jonathan said as he waited for his boss to approach. "But we did get all the frames made for the builder's contract. That is something to be praised."

Brent chuckled. "For a while there, I didn't think it was going to get done. I sure appreciate your team staying late on Wednesday night."

"I always appreciate the overtime. Plus, things are crazy at my house. I didn't mind escaping things for a bit."

"Why are things crazy? Because Winnie's gone?"

"Yes, but that's not all. We are hosting church this weekend."

"Already?"

Jonathan appreciated how Brent took the time to get to know their ways. "*Jah*, it's been a year since we hosted last. It just feels like it happens more quickly."

Brent slapped Jonathan's shoulder. "Best of luck with that. I have some time tomorrow, do you need help unloading the benches?"

"Eli and Henry are coming to help. But I thank you just the same."

"Well, good luck. I'm going home with my fingers crossed. What do you think my chances are that Tricia has dinner ready?"

Jonathan chuckled. "Slim to none." Brent's wife was a teacher. It was standard practice for Brent to take her out on Friday nights. "You best plan to get gussied up and take her out. She'll be mighty pleased with that suggestion."

"Spoken like a man who's been married before," Brent said with a grin. "I'll definitely take her out. See you Monday, Jon."

Jonathan waved him off. As he watched Brent practically scamper to his car, he tried to recall the last time he'd eagerly run home. He couldn't remember.

Oh, he loved his girls, and he was always eager to spend time with them, but that wasn't the feeling he longed to experience.

But moments later, as he and Blacky were making their way home, Jonathan found himself thinking of Katie once again. Perhaps she'd made pork chops or a roast. Katie was a mighty fine cook.

But her skills in the kitchen were not what he kept thinking about. No, it was her sunny nature. The way she smiled tenderly at Hannah.

The way she greeted him when he walked in the door—just like he was worth waiting for. With that in mind, he found himself spurring Blacky on. He'd been waiting all day to see her, as well.

Chapter 11

"I don't know if I'll ever be able to move again," Katie moaned as she finally sat down at the kitchen table after a number of the folks had left Jonathan's home from the church service. "Every bone in my body aches. Jonathan, try not to trip over me tomorrow morning when you wake up."

"I canna promise you that. The way you are sprawled out, why it would make a man have a difficult time getting around you."

With effort, Katie pulled a foot in so it rested under the table. "Better?"

Jonathan pretended to have a difficult time squeezing through the opening. "Only a bit," he said, sucking in his stomach comically.

Katie couldn't help but notice that he didn't have much of a stomach to tuck in. No, Jonathan Lundy was all solid muscle, and that was the truth. But no matter how attractive she found him, there was certainly no way she could let him—or anyone else in the room—see that. "How's this?" she asked, pulling in her chair a bit more. But in her soreness, the feet of the chair only moved an inch or so in.

He took things into his own hands and merely pushed the chair forward, then walked around her easily. "This is much better, now."

As everyone around her chuckled, Katie did her best to not let everyone see how drawn to Jonathan she was.

When she'd first arrived, he'd seemed terribly aware of her, yet emotionally distant. But things had changed during the last two weeks. Little by little, he'd unbent enough for Katie to see glimpses of the warm person underneath the distant manner. This playful attitude drew her to him even more than his handsome looks.

Blissfully unaware of her feelings, Jonathan walked passed her and joked some more. "If I would've known a simple church service was going to wear you out, I would've asked for more help."

"I did just fine."

The laughter in the room rose again. "He has you there, Katie," her mother said, her voice merry. "If you complain much more, we'll all think preparing for services was too big a job for you. You might have to get up, after all."

"*Jah*. Otherwise, you will be covered in foot-prints." With a wink toward Anna, *Daed* said, "And you would dirty your new dress."

Katie sat up and smiled at her father. "Well, I certainly don't want that to happen." With only a bit of a wince, she stood up and faced her family. "I can't believe how worried I was about today. *Mamm*, even though I helped you prepare the house for church many a time, I never fully understood why you would get so short-tempered with us just hours before everyone was due to arrive. Now I know."

"I was never short-tempered."

Henry folded his arms across his chest. "No, *Daed* always spent most of his time in the barn during preparations for no reason at all."

"Well, maybe I was a bit cross."

"Only a bit, Irene," Katie's father said with a smile.

Jonathan perked up. "I think Katie did a fine job. We had a lot of people here, and everyone enjoyed both the worship and the luncheon. Our house looked neat and shiny clean, as well. You did all of us proud, Katie."

Katie beamed at the praise. Though she felt as if she could sleep for a week, she also was terribly pleased with how well everything turned out. Of course, none of it could have gone so well if not for the many hands that worked together. Over the last three days, the Lundy home had been full of women helping to clean the kitchen, prepare the meal, and help tend to the walkway. Cabinets shone and the oak floor gleamed.

"*Danke*, Jonathan, but we know it took many people to make today a success." Looking around the room, she added, "I know I would have burst into tears yesterday if not for knowing that all of you were working by my side."

"Hosting one hundred fifty people is a lot, no matter how prepared you are. I, for one, am glad that we will not be hosting next," her mother said.

"Me, too. I was so nervous about making sure everything was perfect that I thought I was going to get sick," blurted Anna. Then, as she realized how she sounded, she looked around the room. "I hope that's okay to admit?"

"Only among family and friends," Eli teased. He rocked back on his heels. "And speaking of family, I think I'd best get going. I promised my nephews I'd play basketball with them later."

As he walked to the door, Eli scanned the group of them again. "It's just a shame that Winnie wasn't here, you know? It didn't feel the same."

As the door shut behind his friend, Jonathan nodded, his features far more reflective. "I have to admit to feelin' the same way. I want Winnie to be happy, but it is difficult to imagine her not being here in the future. I hate the thought of her always living in Indiana."

"If it's any consolation, I can tell you that I've found that worrying and second-guessing makes no difference," Katie said softly. "People will do what they will. All we can do is hope their decisions are good and that they made their choices with both their head and heart."

"That is good thinkin'. I'll pray that Winnie is thinking that way."

As was the norm, the adults took time to relax and enjoy each other's company while the *kinner* bundled up, played outside, then ran into the kitchen and asked for snacks. As the hours grew late, toddlers found places to nap in back bedrooms and older members found themselves nodding off.

As the sun set, families hitched up their buggies and began to leave. More friends waved good-bye, promising to stop by later in the week to help load pews into the wagon.

At last only Katie's family remained. Happy for Anna's and her mother's company, she used the opportunity to show off the progress Mary and Hannah were making with the quilt. Attentively, she listened as her mother offered additional suggestions for more simple projects.

However, no matter who was at the house, Katie was constantly aware of Jonathan. His soft, distinctive voice echoed to her whenever he spoke. Every so often, she'd find her eyes straying to him, noticing how handsome he looked in his cornflower blue shirt. She smiled when he laughed with the other men in front of the fire.

She couldn't help but notice that Jonathan also seemed to be looking her way more than once or twice. He'd hurried to help her when she'd carried a load of quilts to spread out for the children. He clasped her elbow when she almost stumbled on a step.

Most of all, he seemed to be enjoying himself. That had to mean things were getting better between them. Perhaps they'd set the groundwork for a future together.

Perhaps her dreams of sharing a life with him weren't so far-fetched, after all?

"I can't help but feel sorry for Winnie," Jonathan said to Katie two days later as he folded up his sister's latest letter. He'd brought it inside with him when he came home from work, but had waited until after their dinner of pork roast and stuffing to read it.

Katie and he were now enjoying carrot cake and coffee and discussing the letter. "Though I tried to warn Winnie about the dangers of getting her hopes up, I feel bad that things aren't turning out like she'd hoped."

Katie felt the same way, as well as a little bit dismayed. The practical part of her had always assumed Winnie would be returning with wedding plans. After all, such a forthcoming agreement must had been understood between Winnie and her Malcolm, otherwise, why would Winnie have been so all fired up to go?

Now, though, Katie realized that she'd been just

as swept away in Winnie's flights of fancy. "Perhaps she needs to be a bit more patient. It takes time to plan a future. Winnie must know that."

"She might. This Malcolm may not be so sure." He speared another chunk of cake. "And if he's not sure about Winnie, then it is best she finds out now. He'd have to go a fair distance to be good enough for my sister." Warming up to the subject, he added, "Winnie's got a lot to offer, don't you think?"

"Indeed," she said, smiling as Jonathan scooped up another bite of cake. Oh that man did enjoy his sweets!

"I think she's mighty pretty. Don't you think so?"

"I do." Winnie was tall and slim and willowy. She handled herself well, too, walking proudly, never timidly among their people. Katie had a feeling that if Winnie were dressed like an *Englischer*, she'd catch the attention of quite a few people.

"*Jah*? That's it?"

"I don't know what else to say. Yes, she's pretty." Sometimes Jonathan's manner was so like Henry's that they could be twins. Henry, too, had always been protective of her and her feelings. Feeling sorry for him, she finally added, "Brothers always feel protective of their sisters though. I'm not sure if you would see her flaws, if she had any."

After scraping the last of the plate for a smidgen of frosting, he chuckled. "Your words are fair." Pushing back his chair, he stood up. "Well, anyway, perhaps it is just as well, then. He doesn't seem to understand how much she would be giving up to be his wife. And, if he's not aware of that, then he surely doesn't sound like the man for her."

"Who knows who that will be?"

"Well, not someone like Malcolm sounds to be. We've now received ten letters from Winnie. She doesn't mention Malcolm doing much other than working at the hardware store."

Katie found she had to agree. "I'm sure Winnie is wondering why he invited her out to see him, if he isn't making any time for her. When I wrote to her last week, I encouraged her to hint to him that she'd enjoy going for walks or visiting the shops around his home."

Tapping on the latest letter, Jonathan frowned. "If he's done any of that, we haven't heard about it. Yes, this Malcolm is definitely not the right man for Winnie. I do not think they would make a good match of it. Poor Winnie. I wonder what she'll do now. Maybe she should just hurry home."

Though Jonathan seemed to be talking to himself, not her, Katie wondered the same thing. Winnie wasn't afraid to speak her mind, even to the men and elders of their order.

And though she was loyal to a fault and a hard worker, Katie had always sensed a slight dissatisfaction in her, as if she wasn't quite sure what she was unhappy about, but it was there all the same. Though no one in their circle of friends had ever openly commented on it, Katie had spied knowing looks between other girls when Winnie blurted out something that was slightly too brash.

She didn't look much like the rest of them, either. Her hair was a dark, dark brown. Almost black. The opposite of Jonathan and his light, almost golden head of hair. Her light blue eyes warred for attention with her dimples. More than one man had commented on them.

But underneath her striking looks and strong personality was a warm heart just begging to be loved and nurtured.

Katie was sure that with the right love and affection, some of Winnie's armor would melt away, leaving just a gentle heart and sweet nature for all to see.

Eli had been right when he'd stated that it had been strange not to have Winnie around. She added a lot to every conversation and her fun laugh was infectious.

But by the sound of Winnie's letters, Malcolm didn't see any of that. Or if he did, he wasn't sharing his thoughts with Winnie.

Tracing one calloused finger along the crease in the letter, Jonathan frowned. "Katie, I feel mighty responsible for her plight. I should have known better than to let her go off to Indiana like she did."

"You had no choice." Giving into impulse, Katie reached out and patted his arm. "Malcolm couldn't come here, not with his father doing poorly and the hardware store his sole responsibility. You had to let her meet him. She is old enough, too. Old enough to know her own mind."

"*Jah*, but perhaps I should have asked her not to stay for so long."

"Everyone thought his family sounded amiable and kind. We all assumed she'd be happy."

"But I could've said no."

"If you'd done that, there would have been trouble, too. After all, she's your sister, not your daughter."

"It is still my duty to protect her."

"But isn't it also your duty to be there for her even during difficult times?"

"But this was of her own making. Now she's hurting. I could have prevented this."

"I disagree. She did not bring this disappointment on herself, it was just how things worked out."

He pushed his dessert plate to one side. "But I should have known."

"How could you?" Because she felt she had some knowledge on the subject, Katie said, "Winnie had to take a risk in order to be happy. She had to do something for herself, just to see if she could. She had no choice, don't you see?"

"Not at all. There's plenty of men here for her."

"Then why hasn't one taken her fancy?"

Jonathan shook his head. Katie knew even if he did have some ideas, he would never say anything. His loyalty to his sister would never permit that. More softly, Katie said, "Jonathan, Winnie has only done what she intended. She wanted to get to know Malcolm and his family better. She's gotten to do that."

"But it hasn't worked out well."

"Jonathan, you're going to have to come to terms with the fact that Winnie wants to have her own life—not just help you with yours."

Like the flip of a page, his expression shuttered. "You make it sound as if I've made her stay here. That is untrue."

He might never have said the words, but Katie knew the Lundy family well enough to know that it had been expected. She would have expected as much out of her family. But she could also see that she'd just inadvertently hurt his feelings. "I'm sorry I spoke out of turn."

But if Jonathan heard, he didn't give notice. "Winnie has never said I asked too much of her."

His sharp tone made her retreat further. "Yes, I . . ."

"You have no idea what it has been like," he added quickly. "Losing Sarah. Trying to raise two girls. Realizing that my days of farming are over, at least for a while. Learning a new trade at the lumberyard."

She felt terrible. "You're right. Sometimes I talk without thinking."

He stood up. "I'd say you do that a fair amount. I mean, you really have no idea about what it is like, to have to worry about other people, do you?"

"That's hardly fair, Jonathan. I may not have children, but I am part of a family. I worry about them."

"It is not the same."

"All right." She felt his hostility like it was a tangible thing, especially since it brought forth all those guilty feelings about Brandon that she'd done her best to keep hidden. Maybe Jonathan was right. This was *Jonathan*. The man she'd secretly yearned for ever since she saw him standing alone during church.

This was the man she'd fought her parents to see, the man she was finally getting to see on a regular basis.

But no longer was she willing to simply just have him. No, she wanted him on an equal basis. She wanted him to desire her in his life not because she so obviously wanted to be there, or because his girls were taken care of, but because of who she was. Inside.

"I wasna trying to make you upset. I was only speaking my mind. There's nothing wrong with that."

"You speak it mighty freely in my home."

Now her ire was up. "When you arrived at my

home, hat in hand, you neglected to tell my parents that in addition to care for your daughters, you also desired someone to always agree with you."

"You are deliberately twisting my words."

"Then that makes two of us." Katie stood up. "I'm going to go be with Mary and Hannah."

"I'm going to the *daadi haus*," he said, turning away.

To his back, she muttered, "I didn't doubt you would, Jonathan. Why don't you go on and be by yourself? Again."

His footsteps slowed. "Perhaps I should arrange to have Winnie return early."

Oh, he was so obstinate, once again trying to think for everyone! "If that is what you want."

Without another word, he stormed off. With a scrape of her chair, she left the kitchen, too.

But the greeting of resentful silence in the living room told Katie no comfort was going to be found there, either.

Hannah greeted her with wide eyes. "What did you say to *Daed*?"

"Just something that was needed. . . ."

"You made him mad."

"I know. He made me mad, too."

Just then, Mary appeared from around the corner, a scowl on her face. "Katie, you said you were gonna make things better here."

Katie had wanted to. She'd wanted to befriend the girls and build a relationship with Jonathan.

169

However, every time they took a step forward, two steps back seemed to follow soon after. "I can only be myself, Mary. Your father is a capable man. He doesn't need a woman like me to fix things; he only wanted me to be here for a spell."

"Maybe you should have listened to him."

Katie sighed. As always, she should have done a lot of things. But that didn't excuse his rudeness. And truly, she wasn't about to change her words. She'd meant what she said, and that was the truth. "I'm trying to listen to him. But sometimes, he has to listen to me as well. I can't always keep my opinions to myself. That's not who I am. If you learn nothing else from me, please try and remember that. At the end of the day, we can only find solace in our hearts." Thinking of her running-around time, she slowly added, "Pretending to be something we are not is a thankless task."

Mary folded her arms over her chest for a good long moment. "I brought out the fabric," she finally said.

"*Ach*, good. Perhaps we can pin a few pieces together. Soon, I'll take you to the inn and show you how to work my sewing machine. What do you think about that?"

Their tentative smiles were all she needed to wave them closer.

Chapter 12

"Hello, Mr. McClusky," Katie said when she and the girls entered the general store a week later. "How are you today?"

The proprietor laid his elbows on the counter. "Not as well as you, Miss Lundy. I see you have some great helpers with you today."

"I do at that," Katie agreed, looking fondly at the girls, who'd just stood up a little straighter. "Mary and Hannah are *wunderbaar schee*—wonderful nice helpers."

"We've got some peppermint sticks in for the holidays. Would you two girls like some?"

After hesitantly looking toward Katie, they nodded, then trotted after Sam McClusky. As she watched them walk together, Katie felt an unexpected burst of motherly pride. After witnessing her argument with Jonathan, things were getting better between her and the girls. They'd come to an understanding that she could only be who she was. And, once they realized she didn't intend to replace either their mother or their aunt, they embraced her wholeheartedly.

Their companionship more than made up for all the tension between her and Jonathan.

She was now far less homesick for Anna and the bustling schedule at the inn. Instead, she'd begun to feel pleasure in the many tasks of keeping a good home. Jonathan's home began to feel like her own. Just as important, as she'd gotten braver, she'd uncovered a lot of things about his home that she liked very much.

It was obvious that Sarah had been a good house-keeper. It was just as obvious that Winnie's interests didn't lie in that area. Linens and tablecloths were neatly organized and folded, as were the children's old clothes. Newer items were more hap-hazardly packed away or pushed into cabinets. Over the last few days, Katie had decided to wash and dust the inside of most cupboards and to sort the contents. She felt that Sarah would be pleased with her diligence.

Katie didn't bother to tell Jonathan about her work; it was obvious that he would neither be interested in her progress nor appreciate the efforts it took.

Of course, they didn't talk much at all now. He was still stewing over her comments about his and Winnie's relationship.

But that was all right with Katie. She felt she was growing and changing at the Lundy home. And in all ways, for the better. Now that Christmas was mere weeks away, she wanted to make the girls a surprise, new dresses for the season. There was to be a gathering in a few weeks and she wanted the girls to have something new and pretty to wear.

She'd just pulled out a bolt of evergreen-colored fabric when she felt the unfamiliar sensation of being watched. Slowly she looked up. There was no one directly in front of her. Yet, a shiver ran through her. What was going on?

Quickly, she glanced toward the girls. Peppermint sticks in their mouths, they were chatting with another pair of girls—Corrine Miller and her two daughters—over by the baked goods. Katie knew it would be just a matter of moments before Hannah's sweet tooth got the best of her and she came running over to ask for a cookie.

She pulled out the evergreen fabric again and tried to guess how many yards would be needed for two dresses. She was going to need to ask Mr. McClusky to wrap the fabric so Mary and Hannah wouldn't ask what such beautiful fabric was for.

But oh, what a wonderful surprise those dresses would be on Christmas morning! And, she'd noticed that their robes were a little short and that Hannah's looked particularly worn. Perhaps she could buy them new robes, too? She picked up a pretty lavender robe, made of the softest material Katie had ever felt. Already she could imagine Hannah's look of delight when she wrapped it around herself Christmas morning.

"I hardly recognized you."

Katie almost jumped out of her skin. With a gasp, the robe fell from her hands onto the floor. "Holly."

"Yep. That's me." An unfamiliar bitterness swept over her features. "I'm surprised you even remember who I am. I wasn't sure if you even remembered my name."

"Of course I remember you." Katie fought the urge to hug her. Oh, but Holly looked exactly like her memories. She was still as tall as ever—almost Jonathan's height. Her blond straight hair played off her dark brown eyes. She looked so like the friend she'd had in her faded blue jeans, blue sweater with an embroidered moose on the chest, and boots.

So much like everything Katie had wanted to imitate.

Yet, there was a difference about her, too. Her expression was pinched. Her eyes guarded. A sense of desperation surrounded her like a luminous cloak.

What had happened?

Wondering if her actions were all to blame, Katie bent to pick up the robe, using the moment to settle herself. Around them, shoppers continued to chat and converse. Finally settling into the inevitability of it all, Katie faced the girl she'd hoped to never come in contact with again. She should have known sooner or later they'd meet. "I'm surprised to see you here. Few *Englischers* other than tourists come here to shop."

"You know, it would have been a lot easier for both of us if you would have met me at the Brown Dog. Why didn't you? Are you really that busy?"

"It wasn't that. I . . . I just didn't know what we would have to talk about."

"You have a lot of nerve. We were good friends, Katie." Impatiently, she thrust a clump of blond hair away from her forehead. "I thought we were *best* friends."

"We were good friends, that is true. But, things have changed." Behind her, Katie could hear Sam talking with another customer and the girls and their friends eagerly trying out one rocking chair after another. "Things are different now. I . . . can't pretend I'm not Amish anymore."

Holly shook her head in dismay. "Is that all our friendship was? Just an experiment to see what it was like to be someone else?" Her voice cracked. With effort, she breathed deep. "Is that all Brandon was to you?"

Embarrassed, Katie shook her head. "Of course not."

"Then why did you just take off like you did?"

"Don't act like we only had a simple disagreement. Holly, that last time I saw you, why, we argued something fierce. Don't you remember?" Katie knew she'd never forget the looks of scorn Holly had sent her way. How Holly had told her that she'd never forgive Katie for using her like she did.

The quiet, crushed acceptance of Brandon's face when he had realized that his feelings were far stronger than hers had ever been for him. "I didn't think you would want to ever speak with me again."

"I hadn't planned to . . ."

"I really am sorry for my lies." Katie knew she could never forget their last, tumultuous conversation. They'd been at Brandon and Holly's house. They'd been sitting around, watching TV, doing nothing.

Then Brandon had told her he'd loved her.

And Katie had known that she hadn't loved him. Worse, she realized she'd encouraged his feelings because she'd enjoyed the attention. She'd loved the freedom of pretending to be something she wasn't.

But at that very moment, Katie had known one simple truth—she would never leave her faith.

Holly shook her head. "I probably said a lot of things I should never have uttered aloud. But, I was angry, Katie."

"You had a right to be."

Just as if Katie hadn't spoken, Holly continued. "You lied to me. You lied about everything about yourself. But after all this time, don't you think I had a reason for contacting you?" Folding her arms over her chest protectively, she lifted her chin. "This was the only place I could figure out to find you. I've been having to stand around here, waiting . . . hoping that sooner or later you'd show up. I don't have the time for this. Things would have been a whole lot easier if you'd just met me at the Brown Dog."

"I couldn't. I . . . just couldn't face you. You might not believe me, but I do feel awful about my lies. Holly, what do you want from me?"

"I need you to go see Brandon."

Katie felt the wind being knocked out of her. "You don't understand." In spite of all attempts for control, her voice started to rise. "I can't see him. I'm *Amish*."

"You were Amish when we were friends, too."

"That's not quite true. We Amish do not join the church until we are adults, or close to it. When I met you and Brandon, I hadn't joined yet." Even to her own ears, Katie knew she was splitting hairs. In a quieter tone, she added, "Now that I've joined, I adhere to our customs. I would not feel right courting an *Englischer*."

"I'm not asking for that."

"Then why—" She cut herself off, feeling uneasy. Just a few feet away, Sam was watching them with intense interest. If he got wind of their conversation, it could be common knowledge in no time. Nervously, she cleared her throat. "Perhaps you should leave. I mean, I think it would be best now if I . . ."

Holly gripped her elbow. "Walk with me outside."

"I can't—"

"Yes, you can. I'm not going to wait any longer. Come out, or I swear I won't even try to keep our conversation private. In no time everyone in here will know all about your lies. They'll know for sure you aren't near as sweet as you look. I mean it, Katie."

Holly leaned closer, the look of fierce desperation in her eyes more powerful than any words could be. "I'm not the one at fault here. You have to listen to me. And you have to listen right now. You know I'll do it. After all, I've got nothing to lose."

"I've got to check on the girls first."

Just as Holly walked out, Katie quickly approached Hannah and Mary. "I'm just going outside to speak to an English woman for a moment. I'll be right back."

"All right." Mary was obviously having too good a time to worry about Katie's conversations.

Katie found Holly sitting in one of the rocking chairs that dotted the wide front porch. "So . . . what is it about Brandon that you needed to talk to me about?"

"Brandon was diagnosed with cancer."

Glad for the thick wooden railing behind her, Katie gripped it hard. "What?"

Her expression crushed, Holly said, "He's really sick. It had already spread to his liver by the time they discovered it. He's . . . he's not going to last much longer."

"But surely the doctors can do something? I know of a woman who had cancer two years ago but she's doing fine now."

"This isn't the same, Katie. It's bad." Her voice cracked as she strived for control. "The medication he's on isn't to cure him . . . it's to help with the pain. Some days he doesn't seem to even want to wake up."

Raising her head, Holly looked Katie straight in the eye. "But he wants to see you, Katie."

"Why me?"

"He loved you once. I think he still does."

Katie shook her head. Wanting—needing—to deny Holly's words. "I am not the person he thought I was. He knows that, yes? He remembers?"

"He doesn't care. Don't you see? Brandon just wants to see you again. To make sure you're okay. He's worried about you. Wondered what happened to your life."

"I . . . I don't deserve his worry. I treated him terribly."

"Don't you get it? He doesn't care." Slowly, Holly added, "See, that's the thing about my brother. He doesn't care if I'm not perfect, if you aren't, either. He just doesn't want to be forgotten."

"I never forgot him, or you."

"Then don't let him think you did." Holly opened her purse and pulled out a slip of paper. "Here's the name of the hospital. My phone number's on there, too. Go see him before it's too late. I'm begging . . . I'm begging you," she said, obviously choking on the words. "Even if you don't care about me, please go. Please just care about Brandon."

"I *do* care." Yet, even as she said the words, she felt ashamed. Caring people didn't ignore friends. Not even former ones.

"For what it's worth . . . I'm glad I found you. You look . . . happy."

"I am. I mean, I was." Swallowing hard, Katie held out her hand. "Thank you for finding me. I *will* go see Brandon. I promise I will, as soon as I can find a driver to take me to the hospital."

"Try and hurry." Holly clasped her hand with a hint of a smile, then walked away.

Behind her, the door opened again. "Katie? Katie can we get some pecans?"

Blinking away her tears, Katie nodded. "Sure. *Um,* Mary how about you ask Mr. McClusky if we might have a pound. I've a notion to make pecan tarts with you today."

"All right." Mary looked at Katie curiously before pointing to Holly's retreating form. "Who was that?"

"Her name is Holly. She is a friend of mine."

"But she's English."

"I know." As Mary sidled closer, Katie wrapped an arm around her slim shoulders. "She is."

Just as they watched Holly get into her car, Hannah looked up at her. "She sure is tall. She's as tall as a horse."

Katie chuckled at the comparison. "She's tall, but maybe not like a horse." Though it felt as if her throat was closing from so much suppressed emotion, Katie did her best to smile comfortingly. "She's nice, too."

"She looked sad."

"She was tired I think." After smoothing back a nonexistent strand of hair back into her *kapp*, she added, "She . . . she has a lot on her mind."

"Oh." Turning away from Holly's retreating form, Hannah said importantly, "I'm gonna go ask for pecans so we can bake today."

Later, as she walked the girls to the buggy, Katie realized that Holly had finally accomplished what she'd set out to do . . . she'd found Katie and brought up the past.

Now it was Katie who had to figure out what to do with her future.

Chapter 13

"I saw Katie, Brandon," Holly blurted the moment Brandon woke up from his nap. "She finally went to that general store I told you about."

It took her brother a few moments to focus on her. More time passed before he spoke. "What happened?"

"I talked to her."

"A-a . . . and?"

He looked worse. As she pressed the remote control button so he could sit up, Holly used the time to school her features. The nurses had warned her he was having a bad day. His sluggish words and dark marks around his eyes showed they hadn't exaggerated.

"Hol?"

Taking a deep breath, she mentally attempted to moderate her feelings. The last thing Brandon needed was to see her stress. "Oh, well, at first I couldn't believe that it was actually Katie. She was standing with two little girls and all dressed in Amish clothes."

"Two girls? Is she married?"

"No, I later found out that she's just watching them."

"How did she look?"

"Different. Her dress was a violet-blue. It was pretty, but hung loose. Some kind of black apron was pinned over that. Her hair was all twisted and pinned up under a sheer white little hat."

Brandon shook his head. "No. How did she *look,* Holly?"

He still cared so much. "She looked different. But, pretty, too. She looked happy. Well, she did until she saw me." In a cross between a chuckle from the memory and a sob that threatened to erupt from seeing the condition her brother was in, Holly tried to find the words to describe Katie's face when she saw her.

Maybe a cross between utter dread and complete

surprise? "Anyway, we talked. She . . . apologized, Brandon."

"She feels guilty."

"I imagine she does. And she's got a ton to feel guilty about, too. I know you really liked her, Brandon."

"I loved her." Closing his eyes for a moment, he added, "Maybe I still do, in a way."

"I told her you wanted to see her."

He stared at her again. "What did she say?"

"She said she would visit you." She clasped his hand when hope entered his expression. "She promised."

"When?"

"I don't know. I guess when she can get a driver."

"Why a driver?"

Showcasing her knowledge, Holly explained. "The Amish don't drive, Brandon. Most don't even own cars. But they're not against using vehicles as transportation—just as having them as conveniences. So they hire people to take them places."

"You . . . you should have," he said weakly.

"I know I should've." A better person would have thought to offer. But she hadn't. In truth, she'd been so overwhelmed with emotion that she hadn't even given it a thought. All she could think of was that she'd missed Katie, and that she could have used her friendship and support over the last year. Clearing her throat, "Anyway, I'm thinking maybe she'll be here on Monday or Tuesday."

"Maybe." As if the conversation was too much, he closed his eyes again.

"She'll show up," she said with more confidence than she felt. But Katie had to show up. It was Brandon's dying wish.

She'd promised. Holly hoped Katie had finally started keeping some promises.

Late that night, long after the girls were fast asleep and Jonathan had gone back to the *daadi haus*, Katie pulled out her memory box again from under the bed.

After carefully setting the container on top of the pale lavender quilt, she gingerly opened the cardboard top. Oh, it wasn't a fragile thing. On the contrary, it only contained fragile memories. Ones she was both afraid to abandon completely and wary about confronting again.

As she set the lid to the box on the floor, once again the scent of another life burst into the air.

But this time, instead of only recalling the things she'd done wrong, Katie started recalling the good times she'd had. Remembering the laughter she'd shared with Holly. Her first impression of a shopping mall. The sense of freedom she'd felt, just by spending a Saturday doing nothing except watching episodes of *The Brady Bunch* on Holly's television.

Oh, how she'd enjoyed that show.

Finally, she recalled how torn up she'd been

inside, wondering what God planned for her future. Wondering what the right path was to take. She'd been so confused, she'd sought out Henry, though he hadn't been in the best spirits, either. Rachel had left him for an *Englischer* just weeks before.

She'd found him in his workroom, supposedly sanding an old trunk they'd found in the attic. In actuality, all he'd been doing was sitting with his dog, Jess.

"Henry, are you ever going to smile again?"

He'd looked at her and scowled. "Leave me alone, Katie."

"I truly am sorry about Rachel."

He shrugged. "It's not your worry."

"But it is. Don't you know how I worry about you?" She'd swallowed hard. What she'd really wanted was for him to see how she still needed him. She still needed him to worry about her, to offer her guidance.

But Henry was so good. He would never understand her willfulness. Her dreamy nature. Her impulsiveness. He'd never understand her ever even thinking about living among the English.

Absently, Henry rubbed Jess's side. "I'm glad you care. If I was to admit the truth, I'd guess I'd tell you that I'm sorry Rachel wanted someone else. Wanted a different way of life."

"Did she ever tell you why?"

"Why?" He paused to consider her question. "I

don't rightly know. I don't think Rachel was running from me in particular, though maybe she was. Maybe she wasn't even running from anything." Picking up his sandpaper, he rubbed it against the side of the trunk once. Twice. "More likely, I think Rachel was running to something else. To another man."

Reaching down, he rubbed Jess's neck. The dog thumped his tail in bliss. "Rachel was in love. I can't fault that, you know? When a person is in love, there isn't much choice. If you don't follow your heart, then the rest of the world isn't as right. It's like everything is off-kilter."

Katie had been mesmerized by his words. Henry had sounded so wise. And he'd spoken directly to her heart.

And that's when she'd known the truth—she didn't love Brandon.

That conversation had spurred her decision, but had also fueled her regrets. Katie imagined anyone would feel as she did—it was hard to not love someone when they wanted you to. Sometimes, no matter how much you wanted to love someone, those feelings just never surfaced.

Now that time had gone by, Katie knew she'd made the right decision. Yes, she could have handled things far better. But if she had to go back and live her life again, she knew she wouldn't choose Brandon over Jonathan. She wouldn't choose to live a different way.

She had the Lord and His watchful ways to thank for that.

He certainly had guided her through many rough patches. Now she needed His guidance once again. She needed to make things right with Holly. To ask for Brandon's forgiveness. To move forward. To run to something. To run to the path that was meant just for her.

Closing her eyes, Katie said a prayer from Psalm 105 that had always brought her comfort. *Seek the Lord, and his strength; seek his face evermore.* "Help me, Jesus. Help me know what to do, help me know what the right thing to do would be."

With bated breath, she waited for a sign that He heard her words. Waited to feel a new sense of peace. But nothing came.

The wind picked up, blowing branches, which in turn scraped against the outside walls of her bedroom. Quickly, Katie closed the box again and pushed it back under her bed. After blowing out the candle, she burrowed down into the covers and listened to the wind, closed her eyes, and prayed with all her heart. In the dark room, she finally confessed to all of her sins. Confessed to all of her transgressions, asked for forgiveness and guidance. Holly's reappearance in her life had made one thing painfully clear.

She couldn't make decisions alone anymore. She would ask God's help and finally do what He wanted her to. Only then would she ever find peace.

● ● ●

The following morning, Katie knew what she had to do. She had to go see Brandon. There really was no other decision to make. He was sick, he had asked for her, and poor Holly had gone out of her way to find her.

The moment Mary and Hannah left for school, Katie donned her favorite blue dress, then quickly slipped on her black cape, hitched up Blacky, and rode to the Dutchman Inn. There were phones there as well as a place to board Blacky for a few hours. Once she arrived at the inn, she could either ask if there was a driver available, or she could contact one of the people she knew who made a living out of doing such work.

Luckily, Katie didn't come in contact with much traffic on the small, winding roads that led to the inn. The few cars that did pass her waved before slowly making their way around her buggy. She waved back and used the time on her hands to think about Brandon. It was hard to think of him being in so much pain and facing the end of his life.

She shouldn't have pretended she'd never known him. She should have been mature enough to at least try to remain friends instead of blocking all memories of their relationship away, hoping they'd never surface again.

All too soon, she pulled up to the side entrance to the Dutchman Inn, settled Blacky, then approached the manager.

"I'm needing a driver today, Mr. Pruitt," she said as soon as she saw the forty-year-old manager working at one of the back tables. Terry was the original owner's son, and he had taken over the management of the popular restaurant when his parents were tired of the day-to-day grind. "Any chance you know of someone here who could help me?"

"Where you going, Katie?"

She pulled out the sheet of paper that Holly had given her. "Adams Community Hospital. Do you know of it?"

"I do. Amy delivered all four of our kids there." He looked at her over a pair of half-moon reading glasses. "Everything okay?"

"Yes. I'm just paying a call on an old friend of mine." Thinking that he might be wondering why Henry or her parents weren't accompanying her, she added, "It's kind of a sudden visit."

"How long do you need to go for?"

"Not long. Maybe an hour or two?"

Terry nodded. "I can take you. Give me five minutes and then we'll be on our way, okay?"

Thirty minutes later, she walked into the main reception area. Terry had dropped her off, promising to return in one hour.

Now she was on her own.

"Excuse me, I am looking for Brandon Norris. May I pay him a visit?"

The dark-haired lady looked on her computer

then directed her to the fifth floor. When Katie arrived at the nurses' station, she was met with a trio of interested stares. "Brandon Norris, please?"

"You Amish?"

"I am." When they all kept staring, she cleared her throat. "I came to pay him a visit?"

"Oh. Sure." A nurse came around the bright turquoise desk, motioning down the hall. "He's in room 505. Have you been to see him before?"

"No."

"Oh. Well, some days are better than others. His sister, Holly, is sure he can hear everything you say, so if he doesn't open his eyes, don't be shy about talking." She stopped at the door. "We've been keeping visits to about twenty minutes. All right?"

She left before Katie could reply. But Katie was glad. She felt so nervous and worried; she didn't want another person there to witness her struggles. Slowly, she turned the doorknob and stepped inside.

And then quickly wiped tears as she saw him.

Oh, Brandon.

When she'd first met him, he'd always seemed so infallible. So bright and strong. The complete opposite of the man in the bed in the dim room. The Brandon she'd remembered had an easy smile, sparkling hazel eyes. An infectious laugh.

The man in the hospital bed looked at least thirty pounds lighter. His skin was sallow and pale. An

IV tube was attached to his left arm. The brown hair she'd admired so much was cut short.

His eyes were closed.

She stepped closer. Recalling how the nurse had said she should talk, she did her best. Surely an apology was the right way to start? "Brandon? It's me. Katie. Katie Brenneman. I . . ." She swallowed. "I heard you had wanted to see me." Only the machines clicked in reply.

Steeling her nerves, she continued. "Listen. I'm . . . I'm sorry. I'm very sorry about what I did. I'm sorry for lying to you."

He didn't move.

She approached and sat down in the cushioned vinyl chair next to him. What to say next? "I . . . I saw Holly yesterday. She told me you were under the weather. I . . . I didn't know."

Slowly his eyes flickered open. Katie inhaled sharply. Now those were the eyes she remembered. Lovely, multi-colored, perceptive. When they focused on her, she tried to smile. "Hi, Brandon."

"You came."

Oh, there was such pleasure in his voice, Katie was sure she was about to burst into tears. "I . . . did. *Jah*."

"*Jah*?"

"I'm sorry. When I get nervous, I start thinkin' in *Deutsche*." She shook her head. "Oops. I mean, I think in Pennsylvania Dutch."

"Are you nervous?"

"Yes." Steeling herself, she leaned forward. "Brandon, I'm verra glad you wanted to see me. This gives me a chance to say that I'm sorry. You know, for causing you pain. For lying about who I was."

"Why did you?"

"I don't know." With a shake of her head, she forced herself to speak more slowly. To choose her words with more care. Brandon deserved that much. "That's not true. I . . . I think it was because I wasn't sure what I wanted. Back when we first met, I was feeling trapped. Restless. I wanted something new. Wanted a chance to be someone else." She chewed on her bottom lip for a moment, then confessed the rest. "But . . . only for a little while."

"And then you went back."

"*Jah.*"

Brandon stared at her for a long moment. "I guess I can understand that." Swallowing hard, he never took his eyes off of her. "You look so different, Katie. My memories of you are so different."

"I know." Self-consciously, she patted her dress. "I think I only wore jeans when we were together. Not anything like this."

"It suits you, though."

Looking at her dress, at her trusty thick-soled black shoes, she smiled. "I suppose it does." She pushed herself to speak some more, to say what needed to be said. "For what it is worth, my feelings for you were genuine."

"Did you ever love me?"

She knew the hope she spied in his eyes. She'd felt it many a time. And though she realized now that she'd loved the *dreams* he represented, not him—she could have never left if she'd truly loved Brandon—she said the words he needed to hear. "I did. Well, I loved how you made me feel. I loved spending time with you and Holly and laughing. I loved the chance you gave me—to just be Katie."

And just like that, he knew the truth. Stark reality filled his expression as the ray of hope faded. And it was as clear in his gaze as if he and Katie had talked for three hours.

He knew.

She hadn't loved him the way he'd loved her. She hadn't loved him enough to risk everything she was, everything she believed in.

With a sigh, he shifted. "Thank you for coming to visit, Katie."

She stood up. "Can I get you anything? Is . . . is there anything you need?"

She felt her cheeks heat as the irony of the situation became apparent. It was obvious he needed a lot of things. But Brandon only nodded. "Maybe some water?"

"Oh. Sure." She poured him a cupful. Standing up, she held it for him as he slowly sipped through the white straw. Then, as if that effort had exhausted him, he leaned back again. When his eyes started to close, she impulsively reached for his hand and held it between her own. "You . . . you are a right *gut* man, Brandon," she whispered. "I . . . I am lucky to have known you."

After another minute, when it was obvious he slept again, she slipped through the door. Quietly, she entered the elevator, felt so in a fog that she was barely aware of the curious looks in her direction.

Terry was waiting for her when she arrived back at the reception area. "Are you ready, Katie?"

"*Jah.*"

"All right then." She followed and got into his car without a word.

The drive back to the restaurant passed in a blur as she thought of Brandon. Thought about how glad she was to have seen him.

And what a shame it was that the Lord would be calling him to heaven far too soon.

Chapter 14

Katie almost cut her finger to the bone when the back door opened without warning at one in the afternoon a few days later. Then, as she saw who entered, her hands got shaky for a whole other set of reasons. "Jonathan."

"Hi there, Katie."

He stood there silently, almost motionless. It

gave her a moment to collect her thoughts. "Is everything all right with you? You're home mighty early."

He pulled on the neck of his shirt. "I am fine. I was, *um* wonderin' if you would like to accompany me to the woods today. I thought I might gather some wood and such for a project I'm working on."

Since she'd been at his house, Jonathan rarely spoke of anything other than the great amount of work he needed to accomplish. However, at the moment, he seemed mighty different than the usual man she thought she knew. Jonathan had a glow about him, and that glow caused all kinds of things to churn deep inside her. "A project for Christmas?"

"Actually . . . yes." His lips twitched. "It's a project for Christmas, to be sure."

"What are you going to make?"

"It's a secret." Walking across the kitchen floor, his dusty boots making a mess on the planks that she'd just swept, he almost smiled. "Can you keep a secret, Katie?"

"Indeed I can." Unable to help herself, Katie blinked once, twice more. Whatever had come over him? Ever since they'd argued about Winnie, things had been strained between them. Mealtimes had been near silent. Could he have finally decided to make amends? "I do enjoy a secret now and then."

"I was hopin' you'd say that. So, will you come even though snow still covers a lot of the land? Can you spare me the time?"

"Why, *uh, jah.*" Once again, his teasing manner caught her off guard. He was such a complicated man. True and loyal. Hardworking. At times, terribly brusque. But then, just like a shooting star in the dark night sky, he would tease and joke. Those comments would lighten his temperament just like a flash of light in the night sky.

To her pleasure, Jonathan continued to grin while the cat held her tongue. "It's a pretty day. *Gut* day for a walk, even through the last of the snow."

"Indeed. It is." It would be wonderful to take a walk outside in the unexpected sunny day. Though it was terribly cold, she'd felt rejuvenated by the brilliant sunshine when she'd gone to gather eggs that morning.

And, of course, she was always hungry for companionship. No matter how she tried, Katie couldn't help but miss the bustling activity of the inn. The constant comings and goings of the guests, the chatter from them and her family as well, the never-ending chores that took up much of her time and left little room for moments of loneliness.

But now . . . suddenly, he was offering—asking, actually—to spend time with her. That was something she couldn't disregard and didn't intend to ignore.

She'd come to realize that no matter what had come between them, the infatuation she'd once felt for him had grown to something deeper and stronger. "I'd like to help you with your project. I'll get my cloak."

When she returned from her room, after slipping on her black bonnet and claiming her thick wool cape, Katie found yet another surprise waiting for her. Jonathan was pouring hot chocolate into a sturdy crock and fastening the lid on. "I thought we might enjoy this after our ride," he mumbled somewhat clumsily.

He was trying so hard, trying so hard to make their trip special, that once again Katie felt flustered. "I'll wrap the crock in towels to help ward out the cold. And maybe some cookies, too? We have jam thumbprint cookies left over from Sunday."

He pulled out a basket. "I could never refuse those."

"And maybe a sandwich and apples?" Katie couldn't forget that he'd been up and out the door many hours before the sun.

"Anything is fine."

After he left to hook up the wagon, Katie put together a haphazard picnic for two, gathered up her mittens, then picked up an extra scarf, just in case Jonathan hadn't thought about keeping his neck warm.

When she finally joined Jonathan outside, she

saw he already had the wagon prepared. Blacky was hitched up, thick blankets were already spread out on the seat, and the bed of the wagon was already organized. An ax with a thick oak handle lay on the floor as well.

"You sure got all of this together fast."

Jonathan tucked his head. "I had hoped you would accompany me."

In order not to embarrass him, she said the obvious. "Preparing for a project—any project—is a big job."

"It is at that."

After settling in, Jonathan clicked for Blacky to go forward. They were off, the wheels crunching over the ruts in the ground, then later crunching leaves, twigs, and fallen pine boughs. Around them, clumps of snow dotted rocks and shady areas, making all the colors of the woods seem brighter. A crisp pine scent filled the air, causing Katie to breathe in deeply. A cold breeze stung their cheeks as the horse gained speed. Katie did her best to burrow under the blankets. Jonathan scooted nearer, sharing his body's warmth.

She looked his way shyly. He looked straight ahead, but she sensed he, also, was noticing the way their bodies brushed against each other as the wagon shifted and swayed. The way everything felt so right, to be sharing a blanket.

It was no exaggeration to say that this was the closest she'd ever been to Jonathan. Though inches of space and blankets did, indeed, separate the two of them, in her mind's eye, they were practically pinned together. Katie couldn't help but cast interested looks his way.

He had always been handsome to her eyes. His face was angular and solid looking. His beard was so light and soft that it always took her by surprise in the summer, when it seemed to fade against his golden tan. As always, his clear blue eyes made her think of a winter sky. He seemed terribly strong and stalwart and solemn, sitting next to her.

Of course, he'd always seemed that way. If Katie was honest—and she was trying hard to be, that was for sure—she could admit that never had Jonathan encouraged her. Never had he given her special smiles or an extra bit of attention.

He'd been polite and respectful. Whenever he came over to the inn, he'd spend most of his time talking with her parents or with Henry. If their paths did cross, he'd usually only nod to her.

A horrible, dark thought entered her head. Though they'd come far in their relationship, there was a chance it would never be the romantic, close one she'd longed for. What would she do, then?

She'd always wanted to be a wife and a mother. Would she be brave enough to set her sights on another man in the future? Would she ever be able to only think of Jonathan Lundy as a nice, pleasant neighbor who she'd helped for a time?

"Katie, I've never heard you so silent. Are you all right?"

"Of course I'm fine."

"Not too cold?"

"No."

"I can get you another blanket. Or we can turn back, if you'd like."

"I can be quiet sometimes, just like you, Jonathan. I'm not always a chatterbox." She hoped she sounded mature and upright. Maybe he would soon see her in a new light, too. "I'm happy to sit silently and admire the beauty that surrounds us."

He glanced her way before replying. "Yes, God has given us beauty everywhere."

Her pulse jumped. Just like that, all thoughts of being forever his friend vanished. Awareness filled the gap. "*Um,* what project are you thinking of? Can you tell me a bit about it?"

"I can. I need wood, you see. I intend to make Mary a keeping chest for Christmas. She's a little young for it, but she's been through so much, I think she will like it fine."

The news made her smile. "That is a special gift, to be sure. Every girl, no matter what her age, likes having her own keeping chest." Katie remembered when she'd received her own trunk. Her *daed* and Henry had worked on it for months, smoothing and sanding and staining the oak until it was a rich, burnished coppery-brown. She'd been so surprised and touched to see it on her fourteenth birthday.

Over the years, she'd put all kinds of things inside. Quilts, candle holders, a particularly fine basket. A recipe box. All of those treasures were currently waiting for the day when she would become a bride.

"I hope Mary will like it. As I said, she's a bit young for such a thing, but I've been thinking she needs something of her own right now. Something that will be lasting and solid."

"I agree. She will love the chest. But just as important, she will love it because you made it for her."

His lips turned up. "I'm glad you came with me, Katie. Ever since we argued, I've felt bad about things."

"I have, too. I can be too outspoken and insensitive to other people's feelings."

"I have not noticed that. As for me, I need to remember to ask your opinions. I've become too used to only taking my own advice. It has not always served me well. We live in a community for a reason. I need to learn to grasp the hands that reach out toward me."

Katie thought that was a fine way of putting it. All obstacles in life would be easier to manage if help was accepted. "Jonathan, if it is okay with you, I'd like to treat today as a new beginning. We have much in common and much to be thankful for. Too much to be constantly bickering."

To her great relief, Jonathan nodded. "I would like that." Shyly, he glanced in her direction. "I would enjoy a new . . . a new beginning for us, Katie. Back when I came to your home, to ask you to help with the girls, I said that I had no need to think about a future, about a wife. Now I realize how wrong that was. Your presence has encouraged me to see the world and all of its glories again. I feel like our Heavenly Father has given me a second chance."

Once again, Katie's heart fluttered. What was he saying? That he wanted a future with her? Or that he wanted another woman as a bride one day?

She gripped the side of the wagon as they traveled across the snow, their path leaving a thick trail behind them. After a few more moments Jonathan halted Blacky and assisted her out of the wagon. Then side by side they tromped through the thicket of trees, stopping and staring at each one and giving it either a yes or no.

Playfully Katie stood in front of an especially tall tree . . . its height was far over ten feet and its branches looked wide enough to fill a whole room. "What do you think about this one, Jonathan?" she asked, all innocence. "Do you think there might be enough wood here for Mary's trunk?"

"Why . . . well, *hum*."

"It's a nice, sturdy tree, yes?"

"Yes." It was hard for Katie to keep her expression neutral as Jonathan obviously struggled to give the tree a close inspection. "It's tall, that's for sure."

"And very full."

After a pause, he knelt on one knee and patted the trunk. "You chose well, but I had in mind something a fair bit smaller."

"I'm only teasing you, Jonathan," she said, unable to keep from laughing. "I know it's far too big."

To her pleasure, he laughed, too. "I was getting worried. And poor Blacky—he would have had a time pulling it."

"We would have had to rig you up to pull, too!"

"I'm glad you don't really want this tree, then."

Her mirth vanished in an instant. "You would have chopped it down if I'd asked you to?"

"Yes. I wouldn't have wanted to hurt your feelings."

Now she felt bad. "Oh."

Almost tenderly, he gazed at her. "I didn't ask you to accompany me just to ignore your opinions."

Her pulse quickened. "You didn't?"

"No." He bent down, brushed some snow off a boot, then quick as a cricket, flicked a bit of snow from a nearby pine her way. "I took you out here to get the best of you, too!"

When the cold, wet snow hit her right on her nose, she gasped. To her surprise, he had the nerve to sound dismayed. "Oh, I am sorry, Katie. I didn't realize a little bit of snow would bother you so much. Henry told me you have had your share of snowball fights."

"Oh! I'll show you! Henry taught me well." Her first throw caught him off guard when it landed right in the middle of his chest.

"How well?" With lightning speed, he threw a ball at the branch above Katie and laughed heartily when a clump of snow landed on her black bonnet.

"Mighty well," she exclaimed. Well, attempted to, around a mouth of frozen slush.

It was every man for himself. Katie formed snowballs as quickly as she could and threw them at her attacker. Jonathan proved to be a very able fighter himself. His aim was true and his laugh merry.

After a few minutes, they both were slumped against trees and laughing loud and heartily. "You surely managed to surprise me, Jonathan. I didn't know you could be so lighthearted."

"I didn't know you could throw so hard," he teased. "I thought you'd throw like a girl."

"Henry taught me many things. You'd be surprised at what I can do." Lifting her chin, she said, "He even taught me to play basketball."

"I guess we each still have much to learn about the other." Brushing a stray clump of snow from her nose, he added, "I welcome that, Katie."

His declaration left her as breathless as the snowball fight had. "I . . . I do, too." Yes, their connection felt even stronger now. Katie knew something subtle had changed between them. Tension filled the air as they stared at each other. For a moment,

Jonathan looked about to speak, then, shaking his head, he slowly stood up. "I suppose we better find a suitable tree."

"Yes. We had better." She scrambled to her feet as well. When a clump of snow clung to the hem of her dress, she shook the fabric harder than she intended. "If we don't hurry, we'll run out of time."

The silence shifted again, filling the distance between them with a sweet expectation.

Slowly, they continued to walk through the trees. After a few moments, over a ridge in the distance, Katie saw a buck, its grand rack of antlers proudly displayed. She pointed.

"*Ah,* yes. He is a beauty, for sure." Together they smiled when two other deer carefully moved out of the cover of evergreens and stepped into the clearing. Then, as one caught sight or smell of them, they darted away as one.

"Did you have your rifle?" Katie knew deer meat would last a good long time.

"I didn't need it today. I shot a deer at the beginning of hunting season. Eli and I divided it up—he's making sausage for me. So, I don't need any more."

"I'm mighty glad. I do love to look at their graceful presence."

"I do, too."

Finally they came to the perfect oak tree. It was a homely, rather short and stunted thing, but the trunk was good and solid, and the lines were lovely. With little effort, Jonathan chopped it down. Birds and squirrels around them squawked in annoyance as the branches cracked and fell to the ground with a hefty thump.

Holding the sturdy ax in his right hand as if it was no heavier than a fork, he glanced her way. "Could you hold this for me?"

"Surely." She tried not to show her surprise when she realized just how strong Jonathan was. The ax had to weigh over ten pounds, at least.

Katie then stood to one side as Jonathan wrapped a rope around the bottom branches and began to pull.

By the time they got back to the wagon, Katie felt glorious. Her cheeks burned from the cold, but her body was warm, thanks to the added weight of the ax and the brisk pace in which they returned to the wagon. After securing the tree onto the open back, Jonathan pulled out the basket. "Do you think we could have our snacks now?"

"Of course." Feeling like a child playing house, Katie scrambled back to the bench seat and poured two cups of cocoa into thick ceramic mugs.

Jonathan sipped gratefully. "It's still warm."

Wrapping her mittened hands around her mug, Katie nodded. "I'm glad." She opened a tin. "Cookie?"

"You like to bake very much, don't you?"

She was surprised he'd noticed. "Yes."

"It shows. You are a mighty good cook."

"Thank you. I . . . enjoy cooking." Handing him the tin, she hastened to come up with something else to say. "Hannah was in charge of making the thumbprints in each one of these."

He bit into his with obvious pleasure. "It's been nice to see the kitchen so busy. You have a great way with Mary and Hannah. The girls' moods have brightened considerably since you came."

"I'm glad. I like being with them."

"I know they like you, too. The girls enjoy your company, Katie."

She bit into a cookie to refrain from answering.

But that seemed to be just fine for Jonathan. To her surprise, he even seemed to be in the mood to chat. "Katie, when I first came to your home, when I first came to speak with you, I was only thinking of needin' someone till Winnie came back."

"I know."

"When your father mentioned how they were worried about the two of us being alone, I have to tell you, it took me by surprise. I had always assumed things would stay the way they were. I hadn't counted on things changing."

"Have they?"

"I think so. Yes. Especially after our talk the other night."

"How do you feel now?"

He hung his head. "Well, it's like this. After I went back to my room, I did a lot of thinking. I thought about the past, and what I hope to find in the future. I did some thinking about Winnie, too."

"What did you discover?"

"It occurred to me that your advice made a lot of sense. I can't be responsible for everything that's happened in my life. That's God's job. It is mine to accept and to prayerfully let the events guide me." He paused, as if carefully weighing each word. "I also realized that I can't blame myself for Sarah's death anymore."

His words shocked her. Everyone had known that Sarah's buggy accident was just that—an accident. "I never knew you felt you were to blame. Why do you?"

"She was my wife. I let her go where she wanted to go. I let her drive that buggy whenever and wherever she wanted to. Maybe if I had told her no, it wouldn't have happened."

In spite of the gravity of the conversation, Jonathan's words made her smile. "I knew Sarah. She was a good woman. But she wasn't the type of person to be told what to do, Jonathan. Even I know that. I don't think she would have listened to you if you had told her no."

"I think I finally have come to believe that, too." After sipping the last of his drink, he set the mug down. "Yes, it is definitely time for me to move forward. And that is why I think it is time that we came to an agreement."

With shaking hands, Katie set her mug down as

well. Was this what she thought it was? "An agreement?"

Jonathan's face couldn't have been more beet red. "I've seen how wonderful good you would be for our family. I see that there is much I've been missing. You are perfect for the girls. Mary and Hannah need a woman like you—a person of honor and goodness to look up to."

That was all fine and good. Katie did, indeed, want to be a good mother to the girls. But love from two little girls wasn't all she needed. She needed love from their father, as well. "And you?" she whispered. "What . . . what do you need?"

"I need a wife."

"I see."

"Any man would be happy to have a wife like you, Katie."

His words weren't enough. She wanted them to be. She wanted to be excited about a life with him. But in her heart, Katie knew she had to have love. Otherwise, how could she ever live with her regrets about Brandon? She could have had a life with Brandon, but she'd refused to marry someone she didn't love with all of her heart.

Now, here, the opposite was happening. She could have the man she loved, but she wouldn't have his heart.

The irony of it all—the frustration of it all—made her want to burst into tears. When was it ever going to be her time? When would she ever find a relationship that was equal and meant to be?

Of course, she could never bring up all of that to him.

Neither could she tell Jonathan about Brandon. After all, what would he say if he ever learned just how close she'd been to leaving their order? What would Jonathan say if he knew that she'd made many mistakes? That she'd taken advantage of Holly's friendship because she wanted freedom. Because she'd wanted to know how it felt to have an English boy like her.

What would Jonathan say if he found out she was not as near as complacent as she'd led him to believe? Would he still want her?

Of course he wouldn't.

Just as important, what would happen if he never found out about her *rumspringa*? Could Katie face a future filled with secrets?

She quickly sipped her hot chocolate to keep from answering.

Yet, he noticed her dillydallying. "Katie, do you have an answer for me?" Scanning her face, he added quickly, "I intend to speak with your father, of course, but I was eager to speak with you first."

She couldn't give him an answer. Not yet. It was hard to wrap her mind around his proposal. The moment felt so different than how she'd always imagined it would be.

Did she even love him? Or was Jonathan Lundy yet another "goal" she'd tried to attain?

To even think such a thing felt wrong.

Against her will, she thought of Brandon. He'd freely confessed his feelings for her. She'd known in an instant that she needed to get away from him. It wasn't right to use his feelings.

But . . . Jonathan hadn't mentioned love.

"Katie, must you make me wait so long? The question wasn't a hard one."

But that was the problem, wasn't it? It was a terribly hard question for her to answer. "Jonathan . . . I am not without faults," she said slowly.

"I know that. I have my faults, too. None of us is without sin."

She shook her head. "No, that is not what I'm trying to say."

Cool blue eyes met hers. "What are you trying to say?"

Here was her chance. She could tell him everything. Then she would know if he loved her enough to overlook her past and her faults. Her burdens would be gone and she could start anew.

But just as she opened her mouth to do that, all the words stuck in her throat. With some bit of disappointment, she realized she couldn't do it.

She wasn't as strong and stalwart as she'd always hoped to be. She was too afraid of rejection. Too afraid to make a lifelong mistake. "I . . . I mean . . . I need to think about this. Is that all right?"

"Oh. Well, *um, jah,* sure. If that is what you want."

Katie could tell he was disappointed. She was saddened, too. She was disappointed in herself, and, to a certain extent let down by his proposal. She'd hoped for more words of love and caring. Less about duty and her ability to care for his daughters.

She felt choked by the many complicated feelings rolling inside her, and the many harsh truths she had learned about herself.

Slowly, they put away the picnic supplies and settled in for the long ride home. As the breeze picked up, Katie looked around at her surroundings. No longer did the snow-covered ground look magical. No longer did the air feel invigorating and crisp against her skin.

Now she just felt cold.

Jonathan motioned Blacky forward. Without complaint, the sturdy workhorse plodded forward, the weight of the heavy tree not seeming to be a burden. They were on their way home. But this time, instead of moving closer for warmth, they spread farther apart, in accordance with the emotional distance each was feeling.

The cold wind no longer felt fresh and bracing. Instead it burned her cheeks and stung. Her clothes suddenly felt damp and frozen from their snowball fight.

Inside, she felt empty and hollow. She breathed deep and hoped tears wouldn't fall; she wouldn't know how to explain them.

Chapter 15

Two days had passed since Jonathan almost proposed. During those forty-eight hours, Katie's feelings had run a gamut of emotions. At times she felt as elated and buoyant as a new day. Other times she felt sure her life had come full circle and she was in a mighty dark place, indeed.

Had Jonathan's offer really been a proposal? Or had it been merely an offer to form an agreement of some sorts, in order to keep things the same? Jonathan didn't seem to make any spur of the moment decisions. Katie doubted he offered marriage without careful consideration of what it would mean to his future.

What would it mean for her future? She was capable of taking care of Mary and Hannah. She could cook and sew, and Jonathan had thought she was companionable. Once again, she remembered watching him just weeks after Sarah's funeral and wishing she could do something—anything—to bring him comfort. She'd felt so sorry for him. So sorry for his loss.

Back then, when she closed her eyes after her evening's prayers, she'd think about Jonathan. She'd wonder if Rebekeh had been right, that Jonathan would never wish to marry again. But then, she'd also dare to dream that maybe he would. That maybe he would one day look at her differently. With wonder and yearning. Of course time spent getting to know Jonathan had changed some things. Now she no longer thought of him as just a man who needed help and a partner. She no longer just hoped for his attention. She no longer imagined him without flaws, and therefore above her reach.

Instead, she knew him for everything he was, both good and bad. Jonathan kept to himself, while she reached out for people. He still had many feelings for Sarah, while she only had feelings for him.

And, of course, he only saw the best parts of her. He never guessed of the many mistakes she'd made over the years.

If she continued to try to be perfect, she would win him, and win the life she'd always wanted. But then, of course, it would come with a mighty heavy price.

It was all terribly confusing. All she knew was that the thought of what she might be settling for brought tears to her eyes. Though Katie had never been especially close to Rebekeh, her older sister had always been far too practical to pay any mind to dreamy Katie, she tried to recall Rebekeh's feelings about love and marriage.

But all she could remember was inevitability. Rebekeh had always known she'd marry as soon as she could. Her lovely, practical sister had been courted, engaged, and finally prepared for the wedding with the businesslike manner of a banker.

She'd never given a single sign of ever having second thoughts or of looking back and feeling regret.

As far as Katie could tell, Rebekeh was still living that same way. Marriage agreed with her. Duty and faith and family sustained her. To Katie's knowledge, her older sister had never thought about any other path for herself.

Maybe that's where Katie had gone wrong. She was too dreamy and had her head in the clouds too much. Her people wanted structure and predictability in their lives. They wanted faith and function and steadfastness.

Yes, Rebekeh would say Katie thought too much. Heaven knows, her mother had said that time and again. Always her father was more direct. "You are not in charge, Katie," he liked to say. "God is, and it is His will you should be following. Trust Him, and all will be well."

Katie, indeed, did trust the Lord's presence in her life. Trusted His hand in all things. But she also felt He was probably too busy with life and death situations to worry about her mixed-up feelings concerning Jonathan Lundy.

Now, though, Katie would give anything for time to re-think the last two days. Though Jonathan hadn't pressed her for an answer, Katie felt the burden of waiting just as strongly as if he was over her shoulder and watching her every move.

With Christmas just one week away, she kept

herself busy with Mary and Hannah and did her best not to think about what could be or what might never be at all. Two days after the girls got out of school for break, Katie bundled them up and took them in the buggy to her parents' home.

Funny how it no longer seemed like it was her place. Instead, it was her parents' now. Yet, when she walked in the kitchen and smelled the wonderful scents of almond and vanilla and the sharp tang of peppermint, and oranges, Katie knew she was once again in her family's tender care. Nothing smelled like her mother's kitchen in December.

Anna greeted her with a floury smile. "*Gude mariye*," she said cheerily. "Good morning."

Hannah giggled at the awkward pronunciation, but for once, Mary wasn't a picture of disproval. No, her lips twitched, too, finally bursting into an encouraging smile. "You learning more *Deutsche*, Anna?"

"I am. Well, I am, slowly. I want to surprise Henry tonight and only speak in Pennsylvania Dutch. What do you think?" Again, the words were awkward sounding and slow.

Little Hannah wrinkled her nose. "I think he will be eager for you to speak in your own English."

Katie would have laughed more if her friend's expression didn't look so crestfallen. "You are certainly sounding much more like us, that is for sure. I, for one, am sorely impressed."

"*Jah*? But what will Henry say?"

Katie knew she'd do her best to find Henry before she left and remind him to compliment Anna, no matter what she sounded like. "We won't worry about what Henry says," she said confidently. "I have a feeling he will tell you soon enough."

Katie spied Anna looking longingly at her mother. "I hope he won't be disappointed. I so want to be a good Amish *fraa*."

Her mother reached out and hugged Anna with a chuckle. "Oh, Anna, what did we ever do without you? You make me smile so much. Dear, don't you understand? Henry wants you, not an ideal woman. And, well, even we Amish women have our faults."

With a wink in Mary's direction, her mother added, "We Amish are not perfect, though sometimes we'd like to think so."

Looking pleased to be included in such a grown-up conversation, Mary lifted her little chin. "We can only do our best," she said solemnly.

"I suppose you're right," Anna replied. As if to give evidence to that, one fierce blond curl escaped from her *kapp*. Hastily, Anna tried to secure it but instead caused two other curls to break free and sprinkle flour over her cheeks and forehead in the process. "I don't want to be perfect. But I do want Henry to feel proud of me."

"He already does, child. We all do."

For the first time, Katie realized she didn't feel a

bit of jealousy about Anna's courtship. Instead, she found herself agreeing wholeheartedly with her mother. "Henry's said more than once that he's amazed at the amount of information you've learned. Our way of doing things can be quite daunting. I, for one, know you will make a fine Amish wife." She'd chosen her words carefully, wanting Anna to be reassured.

"Thanks for saying that," Anna said softly and with a grateful expression. "It means a lot."

"We came to make cookies," Hannah proclaimed importantly. "Can we help?"

Mamm nodded. "Yes, indeed." Wiping her hands on a towel, she said, "If you've a mind to work in the kitchen, you've most certainly come to the right place. Grab an apron, wash your hands, and I'll put you to work. We need to make cookies for us, our friends, and for our guests here."

"We give little cookie boxes to our guests when they stay here during the holidays," Katie explained to the girls. "It's a popular tradition."

Again, Mary seemed to enjoy the grown-up job. "Something *I* make might go to a guest?"

"Yes, indeed," Katie replied. "It is a very important task, this cookie making is."

With ease of one who knew exactly what to do with little girls, her mother gave both girls jobs. Hannah's was to crush pecans with a rolling pin. Mary was put to work rolling out another batch of dough and cutting out stars.

Katie and Anna worked on thumbprint cookies and peanut butter squares, while *Mamm* supervised them all with the ease of many years' experience.

All the while, Katie was caught up on the latest happenings with the guests. It seemed the inn had been even busier than usual, with most guest rooms constantly filled. And, to everyone's pleasure, many of the guests were repeat ones. They greeted the Brennemans like old friends, which, of course, they were.

Katie enjoyed hearing who had gotten married, had more children, or had other special news to share.

"You're going to have a lot of cookies to box and eat," Hannah said much later, after Katie's mother took yet another batch of cookies from the oven and set it on a rack to cool. "More cookies than even all your busy guests could *ever* eat, I think." Still staring at the rows and rows of tantalizing baked goods with wide eyes, she said worriedly, "I don't think everyone at the inn will be able to eat so many."

Katie grinned. Indeed, cookies of all types decorated every counter both in the kitchen and on the makeshift card table they'd set up in the hearth room. Soon it would be time to begin boxing up the treats or there would be hardly any room to walk around, much less prepare the evening meal.

"You'd be surprised," *Mamm* replied. "Many a couple come just to be a part of our Christmas traditions. They know we put our best into those cookie boxes."

Katie laughed. "Girls, one year, we had a couple who only came for dinner and a cookie box. They didn't even stay the night!"

"I would never do that," Hannah exclaimed. "Well, I don't think I would."

By now, Katie knew what Hannah was hoping for. "We might need to help out the guests and take some cookies home for us, Hannah."

"We can do that?"

"Oh, I hope you will," her *Mamm* said merrily.

"These cookies are *wunderbaar*." Hannah sidled up to Katie and exuberantly gave her a hug. Touched, Katie hugged her back.

"*Maam* made cookies sometimes, but not like this," Mary said thoughtfully. "And Winnie isn't too good in the kitchen."

"Oh, I almost forgot to ask you about Winnie. How is her visit going? Has she written you any more letters?" Anna asked.

Katie shook her head slightly, giving her mother and friend a silent warning. Aloud, she said differently. "I think she is glad to have gotten to spend so much time with Malcolm and his family. She is learning a lot about them, I think."

Just as she was learning a lot about Jonathan and his girls.

Though she hadn't realized it before, now Katie recognized that both she and Winnie had been working on fulfilling the same girlish dreams. And, just so, they'd each realized that their dreams were only that—dreams. Paper-thin replicas of what living was really like.

Anna stretched, breaking the momentary silence. "Mary and Hannah, I don't know about you, but I am more than ready to get out of this kitchen. What do you two say we take a break for a bit?"

Hannah's full cheeks puffed out as she peeked into the dining room. "What should we do? Do you have more chores to do?"

"Oh, there are many chores we could do, but I have something much better in mind."

After exchanging a look with Mary, Hannah said, "What?"

"Go check on Katie's puppy, Roman, of course," Anna said. "He's out in the barn keeping Henry company."

Her mother rolled her eyes. "More likely causing mischief. He chewed up one of my shoes last week."

Katie grinned. "He would probably love to play ball with some little girls. Would you like to do that?"

The girls needed no more encouragement than that. Hastily they tore off their aprons and ran to the door. After Anna helped them into their black cloaks, they scampered outside. In a flash they were racing each other down the familiar path.

Katie leaned against the counter as she watched

the girls through the window. Then she turned to her mother. "I'd say we have quite a task before us. We have cookies to box and dishes to wash. What would you like me to do?"

Her mother surprised her by taking a chair instead. "Neither. I'm more interested in sitting for a spell. So tell me, *Totchter*, are you ready to come back home?"

Katie didn't know the answer to that. "Why do you ask?" she hedged.

"There's something a little different about you today. I see an anxious look in your eyes that wasn't there before. Did you and Jonathan argue?"

"No, not exactly. *Mamm* . . . Jonathan Lundy wants to court me."

Her mother blinked. "Are you sure?"

"I am. He . . . he more or less asked me to be his wife."

"Well, that is wonderful-*gut*!" Just as she was leaning forward to hug Katie, her mother paused. "More or less? That doesna make much sense. And, I must say, neither does your disposition. I would've thought such news would make you happy, Katie."

"I would've thought so, too." Nothing was making sense. Not Jonathan's transformation into a reluctant beau, not Winnie's dissatisfaction with Malcolm and his family.

"What is wrong? I thought you had a special place in your heart for Jonathan."

"I did."

"Have you now decided he isn't what you want, after all?"

"No, he is still who I want. I think so, that is." Briefly Katie told her mother about their walk in the woods, and how they'd shared the hot chocolate. That story flowed into others. Before she knew it, Katie was relaying stories about making Jonathan dinner, and how she'd claimed the *sitzschtupp* and was teaching the girls to quilt.

She told her mother about how it had felt to work with Jonathan to prepare for the church services. How Jonathan seemed to be impressed with her industriousness. How she'd spied him staring at her more than once, and how sometimes, in the midst of things, they'd meet each other's gaze and share a smile. Actually, there had been many times that were memorable.

When she was done, her mother crossed her hands over her chest and beamed. "These stories you shared tell me everything I need to know. I'm happy for you, Katie."

But Katie couldn't let her mother think everything was fine. There was a darkness looming over her. Katie was sure things couldn't stay this way. Something was going to happen. Her past was going to be discovered and Jonathan wouldn't want her anymore. "*Jah*, I've had some special times with Jonathan, that is true."

"So why do you hesitate?"

"He didn't tell me he loved me. I'm afraid he doesn't really know me, *Maam*. I'm afraid he thinks I'm better than I am."

Instead of looking shocked her mother merely nodded. "*Ah*. You are thinking about your actions during your *rumspringa*?"

She couldn't lie. "I am."

"I thought you'd worked those things out."

"I had thought I had, too, but maybe not. I made mistakes, *Maam*."

"I know."

"And . . . I thought just being with Jonathan was enough. But now I realize that I want his love, too."

"I've seen him gaze at you when he thought no one was looking. There's feelings there, I think."

Still ignoring the many bowls and measuring cups, her mother stood up and put the kettle on. As Katie watched her efficiently make two cups of tea, she marveled at her mother's self-assured manner. Was she ever going to become so confident?

Returning to the table, her mother set the two cups down. "Marriage to Jonathan is something that you've always wanted. Love is, too. In my heart I think you may find both with him. Give it time, Katie. In time you and Jonathan will find your way." With a tender smile, she said, "Katie, you know, I just realized that you never told me what you said."

"I told him I needed some time to think."

Chuckling, her mother reached out and gave her a hug. "I do believe you have finally learned some patience, Daughter. Praise be to God."

Katie swallowed hard. That, actually, was true. Maybe she had grown up more than she'd realized.

Chapter 16

Contrary to what most thought, Jonathan found he did not mind working in the lumber factory among the English. Perhaps it was because his boss, Brent Harvey, was a decent sort of man who valued much the same things as Jonathan.

Every day at lunch, Jonathan would pull out his basket and eat his sandwiches that Katie packed for him, sitting beside a number of other men who ate sandwiches, too. Manly conversation would flow around them all, which he thoroughly enjoyed. After years of farming, spending most days by himself, he enjoyed the fellowship of other men, the rough and tumble conversations. The laughter.

"Got another trail bologna sandwich today, Jonathan?" Brent asked in what had become an almost daily ritual.

"I do. Three, in fact. Would you like one?"

Like boys in a schoolyard, Brent sat next to him as he pulled out a bag of chocolate chip cookies. "Only if you'll have these in exchange."

"Deal." After a few bites, Jonathan said, "The work is going well today, I think."

"I agree. Productivity is up this year. I hope you'll consider staying with us when spring comes."

"That will be a hard decision. Spring planting is a busy time. And then there's the girls, they'll need watching."

"Winnie will be back then, right? Surely she'll be able to watch Mary and Hannah."

It pleased Jonathan that Brent cared enough about their friendship to remember his sister's and daughters' names. "I don't know about that. Winnie, she's in Indiana now. She might be planning a marriage."

Brent's eyes crinkled merrily. "Congratulations."

Jonathan tried to smile, but failed. "I don't know if a marriage is in the future. But her leaving has made me realize that she needs time and opportunity to follow her dreams." With some surprise, he realized that he wasn't just saying those things. He meant them. When had all of that happened? When had he started living again, and realizing other people had to move forward, too?

Keeping things the same was not the way to go through life. And though he'd attempted to cling to the notion that tradition and consistency was part of who he was—as integral to being Amish as forgoing much of the technology of the outside world—it was likely he'd forgotten that people's needs did grow and change. And once more, it was acceptable.

"Jon, you don't sound very excited about the man Winnie is seeing." After pulling out a bag of chips, Brent popped two in his mouth. "Do you not like the guy?"

"I've never met him. Actually, Winnie hadn't met him face-to-face until she arrived there in mid-November. She'd only been writing to him for several months. But I've been getting the feeling that maybe he is not everything she'd expected."

Brent laughed. "Nothing ever is." After sipping from his can of soda, he added more soberly, "But if Winnie's man is far different than what she imagined him to be, that will be hard to swallow."

"*Jah.*"

"Of course, different isn't always bad, you know?"

"You've got a point, there." Jonathan took another bite and chewed slowly, once again thinking about his life with Sarah. The way he'd struggled to raise the girls on his own, and how he'd come to terms with always being alone for the rest of his life.

It had taken Winnie's insistence to reach her dreams to shake him up.

Because Winnie had wanted to grow, he had sought Katie's assistance. And her role in his life had brought about a whole new barrage of feelings. Now he found himself rushing home to

Katie. He found himself thinking how her eyes had sparkled when she'd tossed snow his way. He realized how often her laugh and her smiles were the focus of his thoughts when he drove his buggy home each evening. Her presence had awakened him to the world again.

Katie Brenneman had caused him to dream again.

Maybe Winnie needed that surge of expectancy just as much. "Maybe Winnie is just having a time figuring out what she wants. Different may be all right, after all."

Brent chuckled. "Love. You know as well as I do that it isn't as smooth as some would like it to be."

The bologna suddenly felt dry in his mouth. "I would tend to agree about that." After marriage to Sarah, having two children, and then, ultimately, losing her and finally grieving her loss, Jonathan had been sure he'd never think about marriage again. He hadn't thought another woman would ever occupy his thoughts again, the way Sarah once had. Boy had he been wrong! All it took was one blue-eyed woman with a resolve of steel hidden behind a sweet disposition to turn him inside out. Taking a chance, Jonathan admitted, "I'm learning time and again that love and marriage isna' ever an easy thing."

"Time and again?" Brent peeked at him under the brim of his ball cap. "What's going on? Have you found someone new?"

"I don't know. Maybe." Jonathan was thankful

Brent didn't say "already" or "again," though part of him sorely felt that way. Things were happening to his heart that made him feel like a young boy again, unsure and scared of saying the wrong things.

"Is she Amish?"

"Oh, yes. Of course."

"What's she like?"

There was the rub. "Confusing."

Brent roared with laughter, loud enough that the other men turned their way. "They're *all* confusing. Some days I never know where I stand with Tricia."

Jonathan was becoming mighty glad to have a friend in Brent. He had never realized that all men had trouble figuring out their wives' likes and dislikes. "Yes, but I thought after Sarah . . ." His words drifted off. It sounded uncaring and petty to bring Sarah into the conversation.

"I've only been married once, but I tell you, my Tricia keeps me on my toes. I never know what I'm doing right or wrong. Just yesterday she yelled at me because I was helping the kids with their homework."

"Whatever for?"

"She said I was doing it wrong. But last week she got mad at me because I never offered to help. Women."

"*Jah. Women.* I fear I'm mainly doin' everything wrong."

Instead of offering advice, Brent chuckled, then patted Jonathan on the shoulder. "Good luck with that," he said before getting up to go to his office.

"*Danke.*"

He used the momentary patch of silence to do some thinking. What had happened, anyway? He'd been so sure he had done the right thing when he'd asked Katie to be his wife.

He was not so blind as to see that she had had special feelings for him for quite a while. But instead of acting all overjoyed, she'd just looked worried and spooked.

Yes, spooked was the word. She acted like he had just found out something about her that was horrible.

It had not been the reaction he'd hoped for.

This was when he missed his father something awful. He wished there was someone who he could reveal all of his hurts and frustrations to. Who would listen to him without rancor and give him direction.

As Jonathan ate the last of the chocolate chip cookie, he suddenly smiled.

Well, of course. Someone *had* always been there for him—Jesus, his Lord and Savior. He'd given Jonathan Winnie when he'd needed help the most. He'd given Jonathan good friends like Brent. Now, He'd brought Katie into his life.

Dear Lord, he silently prayed, *thank you for all the blessings you have given me. Thank you for providing me with a great many people and friends. Please help me continue to follow Your will—and to remember to spend quiet moments to give thanks to your guidance and patience. Amen.*

Feeling lighter in step than he had in years, Jonathan stood up and went back to work. Perhaps things were going to work out, after all.

Chapter 17

Feeling restless in the quiet of Jonathan's home, Katie hitched up her buggy and drove to the inn. The quiet rolling hills and pristine countryside were a sight to behold. The crisp, fresh air invigorated her senses and stung her cheeks.

But not even the terribly beautiful surroundings could stop her from thinking about Brandon.

For so long, she'd blocked out all thoughts of him. She'd also pushed aside all memories of her time with him, sure that her behavior had been so wrong, it was wrong to even recall any of the good times she'd shared with her English friends.

Her recent visit to Brandon had changed all that. His need to see her again, his obvious pleasure to renew their friendship encouraged Katie to recall many moments they'd spent together. It hadn't been all bad, after all. In fact, when she'd looked into his eyes, she recalled the many good times she'd shared with Holly and Brandon.

She remembered the many reasons they'd become friends. It hadn't been all false on her part. On the contrary, most of what they'd shared had been real and genuine, indeed. It had been a mistake to push them away—to not even give Holly or Brandon a chance to make their own opinions about her lifestyle. She should have stayed after telling them about herself. She shouldn't have just expected scorn and anger.

Because she loved her brother, Henry, so much, Katie knew just how much Holly loved Brandon. And because she now understood just how sick Brandon was, Katie knew it was time to reach out to Holly. Holly was going to need all of the friends she could get in the coming weeks. No longer would Katie push someone away because she wished she'd behaved better toward them.

After parking her buggy and playing with Roman for a bit, she said hello to her mother and Anna. But then, still feeling restless, Katie knew what she had to do. With purpose, she walked to the reception desk, pulled out the note Holly had given her, then, before she lost her nerve, Katie picked up the phone and dialed. The phone rang two times before Holly's familiar voice answered. "Hello?"

Katie took a deep breath. "Holly? This is Katie Brenneman."

"Oh. Hi."

Katie frowned. Holly sounded hoarse. "I just

called to let you know that I visited Brandon last week."

"I know. He told me."

"You were right to encourage me to see him, Holly. I'm glad I visited him. It was the right thing to do."

After a few seconds passed and Holly didn't offer any more information, Katie cleared her throat. "So, *uh,* how is he?"

After a lengthy pause, Holly whispered, "I'm sorry . . . I thought you knew, though now I don't know why you would have. He passed away the day after you came."

Gripping the phone harder, Katie felt her world shift and sway. "What?"

After a ragged sigh, Holly said, "I'm sorry to tell you like this. *Um,* it was sudden, though the doctors said not completely unexpected. And, well, he'd been in a lot of pain."

Katie had seen the pain in his eyes. "I'm sorry. He . . . he was such a special person."

"He was. I'm just glad he got a chance to see you. It meant a lot."

"It meant a lot to me, too. When I saw him, I realized how special he was to me. How special you both are."

"I . . . I had thought so, too."

"Is there anything I can do for you?"

"No. You already did what I asked of you. That was enough."

"Would you mind if I called you again?"

"Why?"

Because she didn't want to abandon her again. But because that sounded a bit too much, Katie simply said, "Because I care."

"Oh. Well, then. Sure. Call again if you want."

Gingerly, Katie replaced the receiver. Once again, it felt as if her world had shifted. Closing her eyes against the flood of tears that threatened, she prayed. *Dear Lord, please be with Holly as she grieves. And help me know how to move beyond the past and into my future . . . whatever it may hold.*

Slowly, Katie began to see that He had always been beside her. Guiding her. It had only been her insecurities and fears that had held those things at bay. It was time to tell the truth and face whatever consequences came. Even if she failed.

Even if people were disappointed in her.

Even if Jonathan didn't want her any longer.

Decision made, Katie picked up the phone and dialed Holly's number again.

"Katie? What's going on?" Holly asked.

Before she lost her nerve, she said, "I know it is short notice, but . . . perhaps if you are not doing anything . . . perhaps you'd care to come over this afternoon?"

"What? You want me to come over? To your home?"

"Yes. Well, to my parents' inn."

"Why?"

Holly deserved honesty, even if they never spoke again. Even if friendship now meant that she had to do a very tough thing. "I'd like us to be friends again. I thought . . . I thought you might need me." She swallowed. Oh, this was so hard to say. "I thought you might need a friend, since Brandon is gone."

A moment paused. Two. "You've already apologized. That was enough. I really can't think of anything else for us to say to each other."

"I believe there is more than you might think. Please, Holly? I'd love to introduce you to my family." *Finally.*

After what seemed like forever, Holly spoke. "When, this afternoon?"

"Whenever you want." She felt so relieved, a half chuckle, half sob escaped from her. "What are you doing now? Can you just come on over?"

"Yeah. I've just been sitting here, trying to sort out some of Brandon's things, but I just couldn't do it. Your call came at just the perfect time."

It did feel perfect. It felt like it truly was time for her past to meet the present. "Do you have a pencil? Let me give you directions," Katie said. After Holly's promise to come out shortly, Katie hung up the phone with a huge sense of relief.

"Katie? What are you doing? Why were you on the phone?" Her mother approached, her expression one of concern and irritation. The phone was only used for guests' emergencies and to make reservations. Katie could hardly remember ever using it for herself.

It was time to face the truth. Slowly, she said, "I had an important phone call to make. To Holly Norris. I invited her to come over. She's on her way now."

"Who is Holly Norris?"

"She's an English girl I met during my *rumspringa*. I was once good friends with her. With her and her brother, Brandon."

Her *mamm* put her dusting rag down. "Yes?"

Taking a deep breath, Katie said, "*Mamm*, I have a story to tell you and *Daed*, if you'll let me."

For the first time, Katie saw that her mother was visibly flustered. "This sounds serious. Perhaps we should wait until after dinner to discuss things."

"This is serious. And, *Mamm*, it can't wait. What I have to say can not wait a moment longer. I've waited long enough."

After studying her carefully for a long moment, she nodded. "I see. Well, then, Katie, now is just fine. I'll go and fetch your father."

The hearth room had never felt so cold, even though a fire was blazing in the hearth. When the three of them were seated, Katie gripped a portion of her dress and stood up.

"Like I said to you earlier, *Mamm*, Holly is on her way here."

Her father looked confused. "Who is that?" her father asked.

"She is an English girl I met during my . . . my *rumspringa*." She told her parents about how they first met, Katie in her borrowed clothes. That first visit to the Brown Dog.

"Come now, Katie. There must be more to this story," her mother said. "Why is she coming here now? Why have you never mentioned her before? Is there more you aren't telling us?"

"Yes. During that time, when Holly and I were such good friends, I . . . I saw much of her brother."

"Saw much?" After her parents exchanged glances, her mother spoke. "You'd best tell us the full story, dear."

"When I met Holly and Brandon at the Brown Dog, I . . . I wasn't sure how I felt in my life. Rebekeh was always so perfect. So much more perfect than I could ever be. "

Her father sighed. "None of us are perfect, Daughter. And, I never wanted you to be just like Rebekeh."

"I understand that now. But back then, well, I wasn't so sure about everything. I was mixed up. Emotional. I suppose I was feeling somewhat sorry for myself." She glanced at her mother then. "I know that is shameful."

"But honest. Nothing wrong with that."

"Anyway, out of all the kids I met, two people made me feel like I was a part of their group, Holly and Brandon. I liked being with them. They were fun. They took me to the mall. They introduced me to silly TV shows. I liked Holly a lot . . ." Her voice drifted off. How could she fully put into words her feelings for Brandon?

"What happened, Katie?" *Daed* asked.

"After meeting them at the coffee shop, I went to the Norris house for a time or two. Over time, I grew to like Brandon. Though, not as much as he liked me, I am ashamed to say. He began to talk about future plans. He talked like we would do many things together. That I would always be there for him. And, well, I let him think that." Feeling her cheeks heat, Katie tried to convey why she had let things go on for far too long. "See, it felt good to be wanted. I liked feeling pretty and special."

Her mother smoothed her hands over her skirt. "That is only natural, I suppose."

"It would have been natural, I think, if I had been honest about who I was. But I wasn't."

Katie continued, determined to tell everything about that confusing time. Only by completely divulging her past sins was she going to be able to find forgiveness. "About this time, too, Sarah Lundy passed away. Soon after her funeral, I saw Jonathan and his girls." Remembering that moment, she shrugged helplessly. "Something happened."

To Katie's surprise, her father looked like he completely understood. "You looked at him in a new way?" he murmured.

Katie nodded. "I started thinking about his

family. My heart went out to him . . . I felt sorry for him, but I also started imagining a place for me in his life."

Her mother nodded knowingly. "John, I told you she'd been taken with Jonathan for quite some time."

"Poor Sarah's death meant two things—it shook me out of what I thought was important with what actually was. And it, I'm ashamed to say—gave me hope." Katie hung her head. It was terribly difficult to admit to wanting Jonathan, even back when he was still grieving for his wife.

"One night, I told Holly and Brandon the truth about who I was. And then I left them and never looked back, though what I had done and said weighed on me. Then, just after I went to go help with Mary and Hannah, Holly contacted me again. She sent me letters. I didn't know what to do."

"You should have told us about your worries, Katie," her mother chided. "I could have helped. I could have least listened and prayed with you."

"I think I had to face these fears on my own." Taking a deep breath, she finished her story. "The last time I was at Mr. McClusky's store, Holly found me." Ignoring her mother's gasp of surprise, Katie continued quickly. "She wanted me to go see her brother. He was dying of cancer and had never forgotten me. I went to see him last week." Swallowing hard, she added, "He died soon after my visit."

Her *daed* frowned. "That is a terribly sad story."

"It is. I know Brandon's life was in the Lord's hands, but I do feel guilty for never reaching out to him before. Anyway, now poor Holly is all alone, and I can't let her be. I want to be her friend again, if it's not too late."

"It's never too late, I don't think," her *daed* said. "What you are doing takes courage."

"I don't feel brave, but I do feel better now that I am not hiding secrets any longer." Looking around the room, she felt the soothing comfort of her Savior. "I don't want to be a shell of a person anymore. I don't want to be just the happy Katie who tries hard. I want to be seen as whole . . . even if everything I am isn't so good."

Hesitantly, she looked to her mother. Her mother was the best person she knew. Back when she was sixteen, when she'd thought she couldn't ever measure up, she hadn't even tried. But she'd always wanted her approval. Now she just asked for understanding. "I'm sorry I wasn't what you wanted me to be."

"You are exactly what I hoped you would one day be, child. A woman stepping forward. Reaching out. I like this Katie, I think."

Suddenly, admitting her past didn't feel so terrible. It wasn't shameful anymore. Katie realized those past hurts were about a different person. A person other than herself.

That person had shame and self-doubts and fears about her future. The person she'd become felt different. Oh, she had the same wants, but they were deeper and more meaningful than a mere desire to seek belonging. Now she had a sense of peace within her soul, and the knowledge that no matter what happened, she already had obtained the forgiveness of her Father. And He still wanted her. "Let that therefore abide in you, which ye have heard from the beginning," she murmured, quoting 1 John.

Reaching out for her hand, her mother finished the verse. "That which ye have heard in the beginning shall remain in you. You shall continue in the Son and in the Father."

It was very true. No matter what had happened in their past, everything was going to be all right. The doorbell rang. "That will be Holly."

Her father stood up. "I'm looking forward to meeting her."

As the doorbell rang again, she left the hearth room and quickly stepped across the foyer. As soon as she opened the door, Katie said, "Hi, Holly. Please come in."

Hesitantly, her friend stepped through the threshold. "Are you sure it's okay that I'm here?"

Katie reached out and clasped her hand. "I can honestly tell you that there's never been a better time for you to visit. Please come meet my parents. And then we'll have some tea in front of the fire."

As they crossed the foyer, Katie knew everything was going to be all right.

Chapter 18

"So, you'll forgive me?" Katie asked Jonathan later that evening. After they'd eaten dinner and got the girls settled, she'd asked him to listen while she told him a story.

Oh, it had taken some time. They'd sat in the cozy *sitzschtupp* with mugs of hot tea, and with little fanfare, Katie recounted her story one more time.

Through it all, Jonathan had been silent, only asking questions to clarify information, not to judge her. Katie was mighty grateful for that. But when she thought of how different things could have been if her parents hadn't been so supportive, if she hadn't had Anna, who had already been through so many trials of her own . . . Katie couldn't help but feel blessed.

But so far, this telling had been the hardest, even harder than facing her parents or even Holly. Perhaps it was because she had so much to lose. Katie knew that she wanted a future with Jonathan, but only a marriage and union based on realities, not his imagined ideas about her.

Her worries made her emotions run high. Tears streamed unchecked down her cheeks, though she'd tried her best to keep them at bay.

Tenderly, Jonathan wiped a stray teardrop away with the side of a thumb, then rested his palm against her face, cradling her cheek. "I've told you, there's nothing to forgive."

"Are you sure? I had assumed you would be terribly mad at me."

"Why?"

"Because I've kept so much from you. Jonathan, I know you never dreamed I would've been involved in such things."

Jonathan smiled wryly. "Well, that is true."

Had she lost him?

Tears rushed forth again as she remembered their afternoon in the woods when time had seemed to stand still and so much of their animosity had fallen away, leaving only true, tender feelings. She wished she had thought to keep a reminder of the day for her memory box. That, indeed, would bring her much happiness months and years from now. "I know you wanted someone far more perfect."

But his expression didn't waver. Almost regretfully, he lowered his hand from her cheek and clasped her hands, his two work-roughened thumbs gently stroking her knuckles. "Come, now. We both know that was never true. In God's eyes, we are all worthy of His grace. Do not be so hard on yourself."

"I'm merely being *ehrlich*, being honest."

"I will admit that I had wanted a wife who would make me happy, and who would make my daughters happy. In my rush to do that, I built expectations that could never be met. None of us is faultless, Katie, and, I don't want anyone who pretends to be."

She couldn't keep the surprise from her voice. "Truly?"

"Truly." A bit uncomfortably, he looked at her.

"I don't know what to say."

"There is nothing to say, not really," he said with a smile. He looked away. "I don't want to blemish Sarah's name. She was a *gut fraa*, a good wife. She tried her best and so did I. I just want you to know that I do understand what it is like . . . to keep so much inside."

"Thank you. Your words mean a lot."

"As do yours." Tugging on her hand, he pulled her toward him, so close that their thighs and shoulders touched. "I would be lying now if I did not say that you are perfect for me."

"Still?"

He squeezed her hands. "Especially still."

Katie's heart seemed to stop beating. Never in a million years had she expected to find forgiveness so easily. As their eyes met, a thousand words passed between them, unspoken.

When she remained silent, his lips curved. "You don't have anything to say?"

"I can't seem to think." Truly, she couldn't. What was happening was far more special than any of her dreams or imaginings.

"That's all right, I think. I seem to have enough words for both of us. See, the thing is, Katie, when

I look at you, I see everything I ever wanted. I see everything I once dreamed of having but had given up hoping of receiving."

"I feel the same way."

"Are you sure?" His eyes betrayed his doubts. "I know I've been difficult to live with. I canna promise you a future without problems."

"I never asked for a future like that. I only want a future that is real. That I can count on. And Jonathan, you are not so difficult."

Jonathan leaned close and clasped her hands. "Katie, I have fallen in love with your bright blue eyes and your sweet disposition. I've fallen in love with the way you point out my faults and encourage me to be a better man. I like how you make me smile, and I love how my girls adore you."

At last Jonathan looked into her eyes the way she'd always dreamed he would. "Katie, I want you to be my wife. I can't promise I will be the easiest man to live with, but I can promise I will treasure you always. Please . . . please say you'll be mine. Please say you will marry me."

Katie bit her lip. Maybe—just maybe—dreams could come true, after all. "Yes, Jonathan, I will marry you," she whispered.

And when he leaned his head down to kiss her, and carefully held her close, Katie knew she had just gotten everything she'd always thought she had wanted. Everything she always hoped to have.

And so very much more.

Epilogue

"I canna eat another bite of this wonderful Christmas dinner," Jonathan said to the large gathering surrounding the oak table in the Brennemans' dining room. "You *damen* prepared a mighty fine table, that is for sure."

Katie's mother smiled. "I have to admit to being pleased with how everything turned out. What do you think, girls?"

Katie turned to Anna and Winnie, her two best friends, and in so many ways, the sisters of her heart. One day soon Anna would marry Henry and she would marry Jonathan. Eventually Winnie, too, would find love. All of them could look forward to many years of meals prepared and enjoyed together. "I think it was a fine meal, indeed." More hesitantly, she looked to her sister. "Rebekeh, what did you think?"

"The same as you," she said, smiling in just the way their mother did. "It was mighty fine. Especially since I only brought a pie."

"That was enough this year," their mother said, as Rebekeh awkwardly stood up. "You should be off of your feet as much as possible."

Chuckling, Rebekeh's husband, Olan, said, "I wish you could pay a call on us every day and tell her that. My Rebekeh never seems to want to sit and rest."

"She never did," Henry said with a wink toward Katie. "Though, I have to admit to wishing she would have relaxed more when she was younger."

"Then we could've relaxed, too!" Katie said with a laugh.

Primly, her older sister clucked her tongue. "You two needed me to watch over you. At least *Mamm* did."

As their mother looked at all three of them, she shook her head. "Come, Rebekeh, come sit with me for a bit in the front room. If you stay here much longer, Katie and Henry will tease you even more."

Henry whistled low. "Katie, should we tell everyone about the time Rebekeh made us set the table twice?"

Katie laughed at Rebekeh's expression. "We'd better not. Go sit down, Rebekeh. We'll take care of things here."

Laughter echoed through the inn as Rebekeh followed Katie's directions and followed their mother to the front room. As the men moved to the couches near the fire, Katie motioned to Mary and Hannah to help her carry dishes to the kitchen. "We best get these dishes cleared and washed. They won't get finished without our hands."

"I've got the carrots!" Mary proclaimed.

Hannah rushed to keep up. "I'll carry the basket of rolls."

"Do be careful, girls," Katie called out.

Beside her, Winnie picked up an almost empty dish of potatoes. Katie thought she'd been especially quiet all evening. As they walked far more circumspectly to the kitchen, Katie murmured, "Are you all right?"

"Oh, *jah*," Winnie replied, though Katie noticed that her smile didn't quite reach her eyes. "I am just glad to be home, and am excited about my new job in town."

"I'm sorry things didn't work out with you and Malcolm."

"I am, too." Winnie shook her head. "Oh, Katie, that Malcolm was nothing like his letters. I guess Anna really was right when she said that nothing takes the place of conversations face-to-face. In person, I found him to be difficult and inattentive. I'm verra glad to have my new job."

Almost the moment Winnie returned from Indiana, she'd informed Jonathan that she was going to take a position at the Crazy Quilt. Jonathan, knowing that she was hurting and needed to move on, understood.

Katie had moved back home, but now went to Jonathan's the few afternoons that Winnie worked late. During those visits, she spent time with the girls, fostering their relationship and working on the quilt together. Sometimes she stayed and visited with Jonathan for an hour or two before returning to the inn.

After four more trips to the kitchen, Winnie,

Anna, and Katie were put in charge of sorting left-overs while Irene, Mary, and Hannah carried cakes, pies, and dessert plates to the dining room.

When they were once more alone in the kitchen, Anna said, "Katie, Henry told me you received another letter from Holly. What did this one say?"

"All kinds of good things. Holly has met someone, and even went on a second date."

"I hope she'll bring him over soon," Anna said. "We're going to need to approve."

"Something tells me she'll wait to bring over any of her dates, though she did tell me she wants to come over soon and spend the weekend with me." When Winnie and Anna looked at her in surprise, Katie announced her news. "She wants to make a quilt!"

Winnie burst out laughing. "You'll have everyone you know quilting soon, Katie."

"Maybe I will! All I know is that Holly's letter and good news was a wonderful Christmas present." So was her friendship. That, truly, was what made her heart sing the most.

Jonathan peeked his head in. "Katie, are you almost done? I thought we could maybe take a walk outside for a bit."

His gaze was so warm and loving, Katie felt her cheeks heat. "Yes. I . . . I'm almost done, Jonathan. I would most certainly enjoy a walk with you," she replied quickly, ignoring the giggles of her girl-friends.

Anna playfully bumped Katie with her shoulder. "While Holly's news is wonderful good, I'd say you received a far better Christmas gift, Katie. Jonathan Lundy is mighty attentive these days."

Even Winnie chuckled. "He acts like it's not blustery and cold outside, he's so anxious to be alone with you. We better hurry with the dishes."

Katie hastily rolled up her sleeves with a smile. Yes, Jonathan's love was a wonderful present. He'd given her joy and his family, and a reason to be herself. Most of all, he'd reminded her that by the grace of God, every one of them was blessed and special in the eyes of the Lord.

And that was, indeed, a most wonderful present to receive. . . . especially on Christmas Day.

Dear Reader,

I always look forward to winter. The shorter days and longer evenings provide lots of opportunities to spend more time with my kids. When the weather gets colder, I start baking. I dig out our crock pot and start making stews and pot roasts. Holidays bring opportunities to see family and friends, and before we know it, old traditions will be remembered and new ones begun.

Things aren't so very different in the Amish community nearby. Families there, too, will look forward to many of the same things. Cookies and pies will be baked, special events will be organized, and moments spent with loved ones will be treasured. And their children—just like mine—will eye the evening sky in hopes of an upcoming snow day.

These similarities remind me of Katie Brenneman. She, just like me, has made mistakes that she must overcome. She has dreams she hopes to achieve. More than anything, Katie wants to belong and be loved. I'm very thankful to have been given the opportunity to write her story.

Special thanks go out to my editor, Cindy DiTiberio, for all her help and guidance with *Wanted*. I'm so lucky to be able to work with a lady who is so gifted and positive. I'm also extremely grateful for the many kindnesses of Celesta, the quilting group at our church, to Cathy, Heather, Julie, and Hilda, for reading re-writes quickly and with such a careful eye, and of course, to the members of our small group at church, who couldn't be any more supportive and helpful.

Most of all, I'm thankful for your letters of encouragement and support. I truly love to write, and I'm always excited for the opportunity to work on a new book.

Blessings,

Shelley

Questions for Discussion

1. The theme of "wanting" is woven through many of the main characters in this book. Both Katie and Holly must step outside their comfort zone in order to obtain what they yearn for. Have you ever had to step outside of your comfort zone in order to reach a goal or to reach out to another person?

2. In *Wanted*, both Katie and Holly have close relationships with their brothers. They rely on their brothers for love and support. Holly is willing to do almost anything to grant one of her brother's dying wishes, even putting aside her own feelings. What have you sacrificed for a family member?

3. As the story develops, Katie realizes that the past always comes back to haunt us until once and for all we confront it. In order to prosper in the future, Katie must come to terms with previous mistakes. How do you think she could have handled her situation better? Was she wrong to have kept so many secrets, or do you think the timing wasn't right for her to have dealt with them?

4. Katie's father tells her, "You are not in charge, Katie. God is. It is His will you should be following. Trust Him and all will be well." Have you ever had a situation like Katie's, where it is necessary for you to give up control? How difficult was that to do? Was that the right decision?

5. Katie begins a quilting project with Mary and Hannah as a way to build a relationship with them. What activities do you do with either family or friends that have forged deeper bonds?

6. Winnie learns a lot about herself during her trip to Indiana, even though it wasn't ultimately successful. What do you think about Winnie's trip to Indiana? Was it a mistake for her to go, or do you think it was a necessary trip? Have you ever learned a lesson from a failed opportunity like Winnie's?

7. Do you think Holly and Katie's relationship can be renewed and strengthened, or are they too different now?

8. The Amish take turns hosting church services and a light luncheon. Friends and family help with preparations. Imagine such a tradition in your church. What would be the pros and cons of asking families in your congregation to host a service?

Hidden was SHELLEY SHEPARD GRAY's first foray into inspirational fiction. Before writing romances, Shelley lived in Texas and Colorado, where she taught school and earned both her bachelor's and master's degrees in education. She now lives in southern Ohio where she writes full time. Shelley is an active member of her church. She serves on committees, volunteers in the church office, and is part of the Telecare ministry, which calls homebound members on a regular basis.

Center Point Publishing
600 Brooks Road ● PO Box 1
Thorndike ME 04986-0001 USA

(207) 568-3717

US & Canada:
1 800 929-9108
www.centerpointlargeprint.com